The Young Vigilantes

Also from Westphalia Press

westphaliapress.org

The Young Vigilantes

A Story of California Life in the 1850s

by Samuel Adams Drake

WESTPHALIA PRESS
An imprint of Policy Studies Organization

Westphalia Press
An imprint of Policy Studies Organization
1527 New Hampshire Ave., NW
Washington, D.C. 20036
info@ipsonet.org

ISBN-13: 978-1-63391-087-4
ISBN-10: 1633910873

Cover design by Taillefer Long at Illuminated Stories:
www.illuminatedstories.com

Daniel Gutierrez-Sandoval, Executive Director
PSO and Westphalia Press

Rahima Schwenkbeck, Director of Media and Publications
PSO and Westphalia Press

Updated material and comments on this edition
can be found at the Westphalia Press website:
www.westphaliapress.org

Walter and Bill tramping across the Isthmus. — *Page 132.*

THE YOUNG VIGILANTES

A STORY OF CALIFORNIA
LIFE IN THE FIFTIES

BY

SAMUEL ADAMS DRAKE

Author of "Watch Fires of '76," "On Plymouth Rock," "Decisive
Events in American History Series," etc.

ILLUSTRATED BY L. J. BRIDGMAN

BOSTON
LEE AND SHEPARD
1904

CONTENTS

ILLUSTRATIONS

THE YOUNG VIGILANTES

I

A NARROW ESCAPE

FROM the *Morning Post-Horn*:

"As passenger train Number Four was rounding a curve at full speed, ten miles out of this city, on the morning of October 4, and at a point where a deep cut shut out the view ahead, the engineer saw some one, man or boy, he could not well make out which, running down the track toward the train, frantically swinging both arms and waving his cap in the air as if to attract attention. The engine-man instantly shut off steam, whistled for brakes, and quickly brought the train to a standstill.

"The engine-man put his head out of the

cab window. The conductor jumped off, followed by fifty frightened passengers, all talking and gesticulating at once; while the person who had just given the warning signal slackened his breakneck pace, somewhat, upon seeing that he had succeeded in stopping the train.

" ' What's the matter? ' shouted the impatient engine-man when this person had come within hearing.

" ' What do you stop us for? ' called out the little conductor sharply, in his turn, at the same time anxiously consulting the face of the watch he held in his hand.

" To both questions the young man seemed too much out of breath to reply, offhand; but turning and pointing in the direction whence he came, he shook his head warningly, threw himself down on the roadbed, as limp as a rag, and began fanning himself with his cap. After getting his breath a little, he made out to say, ' Bridge afire—quarter mile back. Tried put it out—couldn't. Heard

train coming—afraid be too late. Couldn't
run another step.'

" ' Get aboard,' said the conductor to him.
' Jake,' to the grinning engine-man, ' we'll run
down and take a look at it. Get out your
flag! ' to a brakeman. ' Like as not Thir-
teen 'll be along before we can make Brenton
switch. All aboard! ' The delayed train
then moved on.

" As it neared the burning bridge it was
clear to every one that the young man's warning had prevented a disastrous wreck, probably much loss of life, because the bridge
could not be seen until the train was close
upon it. All hands immediately set to work
with pails extinguishing the flames, which was
finally done after a hard fight. To risk a
heavy train upon the half-burned stringers
was, however, out of the question. Leaving
a man to see that the fire did not break out
again, the train was run back to the next station, there to await further orders. We were
unable to learn the name of the young man to

whose presence of mind the passengers on
Number Four owed their escape from a serious, perhaps fatal disaster. But we are in-
formed that a collection was taken up for him
on the train, which he, however, refused to
accept, stoutly insisting that he had only done
what it was his duty to do under the circumstances."

Thus far, the *Morning Post-Horn.* We
now take up the narrative where the enterprising journal left off.

While the delayed train was being held for
orders, the young man whose ready wit had
averted a calamity stood on the platform
with his hands in his trousers pockets, apparently an unconcerned spectator of what was
going on around him.   The little pug-nosed
conductor stepped up to him.

" I say, young feller, what may I call your
name ? "

" Seabury."

" Zebra, Zebra," repeated the conductor,

in a puzzled tone, " then I s'pose your ancestors came over in the Ark? "

" I didn't say Zebra; I said Seabury plain enough," snapped back the young man, getting red in the face at seeing the broad grins on the faces around him.

" Don't fire up so. Got any first name? "

" Walter."

" Walter Seabury," the conductor repeated slowly, while scratching it down. " Got to report this job, you know. Say, where you goin'? "

" I'm walkin' to Boston."

" Shanks' mare, hey. No, you ain't. Get aboard and save your muscle. You own this train to-day, and everything in it. Lively now." The conductor then waved his hand, and the train started on. At the bridge a transfer was effected to a second train, and this one again was soon reeling off the miles toward Boston, as if to make up for lost time.

Being left to himself, young Seabury,

whom we may as well hereafter call by his Christian name of Walter, could think of nothing else than his wonderful luck. Instead of having a long, weary tramp before him, here he was, riding in a railroad train, and without its costing him a cent. This was a saving of both time and money.

Pretty soon the friendly conductor came down the aisle to where Walter sat, looking out of the car window. After giving him a sharp look, the conductor made up his mind that here was no vagabond tramp. " It's none of my business, but all the same I'd like to know what you're walkin' to Boston for, young feller? " he asked.

" Going to look for work."

" What's your job? "

" I'm a rigger." And his hands, tarry and cracked, bore out his story perfectly.

" Ever in Boston? "

" Never."

" Know anybody there? "

" Nobody."

"Got any of this—you know?" slapping his pocket.

At this question Walter flushed up. He drew himself up stiffly, smiled a pitying smile, and said nothing. His manner conveyed the idea that he really didn't know exactly how much he was worth.

"That's first-rate," the conductor went on. "Now, look here. You'll get lost in Boston. I'll tell you what. When we get in, I'll show you how to go to get down among the riggers' lofts. You're a rigger, you say?" Walter nodded. "They're all in a bunch, down at the North End, riggers, sailmakers, pump- and block-makers, and all the rest. Full of work, too, I guess, all on account of this Cali- forny business. Everybody's goin' crazy over it. You will be, too, in a week."

By this time, the train was rumbling over the long waste of salt-marsh stretching out between the mainland and the dome-capped city, and in five minutes more it drew up with a jerk in the station, with the locomotive puff-

ing out steam like a tired racehorse after a
hard push at the finish.

The conductor was as good as his word.
He told Walter to go straight up Tremont
Street until he came to Hanover, then
straight down Hanover to the water, and then
to follow his nose. " Oh, you can't miss it,"
was the cheerful, parting assurance. " Smell
it a mile." But going straight up this street,
and straight down that, was a direction not so
easy to follow, as Walter soon found. The
crowds bewildered him, and in trying to get
out of everybody's way, he got in everybody's
way, and was jostled, shoved about, and
stared at, as he slowly made his way through
the throng, until his roving eyes caught sight
of the tall masts and fluttering pennants,
where the long street suddenly came to an
end. Walter put down his bundle, took off
his cap, and wiped the perspiration from his
forehead. Whichever way he looked, the
wharves were crowded with ships, the ships
with workmen, and the street with loaded

trucks and wagons. Casting an eye upward he could see riggers at work among the maze of ropes and spars, like so many spiders weaving their webs. Here, at least, he could feel at home.

II

WALTER'S first want was to find a boarding house suited to his means. Turning into a side street, walled in by a row of two-story brick houses, all as like as peas in a pod, he found that the difficulty would be to pick and choose, as all showed the same little tin sign announcing " Board and Lodging, by the Day or Week," tacked upon the door. After walking irresolutely up and down the street two or three times, he finally mustered up courage to give a timid pull at the bell of one of them. The door opened so suddenly that Walter fell back a step. He began stammering out something, but before he could finish, the untidy-looking girl sang out at the top of her voice: " Miss Hashall, Miss Hashall, there's somebody wants to see you!" She

then bolted off through the back door singing
" I want to be an angel," in a voice that set
Walter's teeth on an edge.   To make a long
story short, Walter soon struck a bargain with
the landlady,—a fat, pudgy person in a
greasy black poplin, wearing a false front,
false teeth, and false stones in her breastpin.
True, Walter silently resented her demanding
a week's board in advance, it seemed so like a
reflection upon his honesty, but was easily
mollified by the motherly interest she seemed
to take in him—or his cash.

Bright and early the next morning Walter
sallied out in search of work.   His landlady
had told him to apply at the first loft he came
to.   " Why, you can't make no mistake," the
woman declared.   " They're all drove to
death, and hands is scurse as hens' teeth, all
on account of this Kalerforny fever what car-
ries so many of 'em off.   Don't I wish I was
a man !   I'd jest like to dig gold enough to
buy me a house on Beacon Street and ride in
my kerridge.   You just go and spunk right

up to 'em, like I do. That's the way to get along in this world, my son."

Walter's landlady had told him truly. The demand for vessels for the California trade was so urgent that even worm-eaten old whaleships were being overhauled and refitted with all haste, and as Walter walked along he noticed that about every craft he saw showed the same sign in her rigging, "For San Francisco with dispatch." "Well, I'll be hanged if there ain't the old *Argonaut* that father was mate of!" Walter exclaimed quite aloud, clearly taken by surprise at seeing an old acquaintance quite unexpectedly in a strange place, and quickly recognizing her, in spite of a new coat of paint alow and aloft.

The riggers were busy setting up the standing rigging, reeving new halliards, and giving the old barky a general overhauling. Walter climbed on board and began a critical survey of the ship's rigging, high and low.

"What yer lookin' at, greeny?" one of

the riggers asked him, at seeing Walter's eyes fixed on some object aloft.

" I'm looking at that Irish pennant * on that stay up there," was the quick reply. This caused a broad smile to spread over the faces of the workmen.

" You a rigger? "

" I've helped rig this ship."

" Want a job? "

" Yes."

" Well, here," tossing Walter a marline-spike, " let's see you make this splice." It was neatly and quickly done. " I'll give you ten dollars a week." Walter held out for twelve, and after some demurring on the part of the boss, a bargain was struck. Walter's overalls were rolled up in a paper, under his arm, so that he was immediately ready to begin work.

Being, as it were, in the midst of the stream of visitors to the ship, hearing no end of talk about the wonderful fortunes to be

* A strand of marline carelessly left flying by a rigger.

made in the Land of Gold, Walter did not wholly escape the prevailing frenzy, for such it was. But knowing that he had not the means of paying for his passage, Walter resolutely kept at work, and let the troubled stream pass by. There was still another obstacle. He would have to leave behind him a widowed aunt, whose means of support were strictly limited to her actual wants. He had at once written to her of his good fortune in obtaining work, though the receipt of that same letter had proved a great shock to the " poor lone creetur," as she described herself, because she had freely given out among her neighbors that a boy who would run away from such a good home as Walter had, would surely come to no good end.

Walter had struck up a rather sudden friendship with a young fellow workman of about his own age, named Charley Wormwood. On account of his name he was nicknamed " Bitters." Charley was a happy-go-lucky sort of chap, valuing the world chiefly for the amusement it afforded, and finding that amusement in about everything and everybody. Though mercilessly chaffed by the older hands, Charley took it all so good-naturedly that he made himself a general favorite. The two young men soon arranged to room together, and had come to be sworn friends.

One pleasant evening, as the two sat in their room, with chairs tilted back against the wall, the following conversation was begun by Charley: " I say, Walt, we've been together here two months now, to a dot, and never a word have you said about your folks. Mind now, I don't want to pry into your secrets, but I'd like to know who you are, if it's all the same to you. Have you killed a man, or broke a bank, or set a fire, or what? Folks think it funny, when I have to tell them I don't know anything about you, except by guess, and you know that's a mighty poor course to steer by. Pooh! you're as close as an oyster! "

Walter colored to his temples. For a short space he sat eyeing Charley without speaking. Then he spoke up with an evident effort at self-control, as if the question, so suddenly put, had awakened painful memories. " There's no mystery about it," he said. " You want to hear the story? So be it, then. I'll tell mine if you'll tell yours.

" I b'long to an old whaling port down on the Cape. I was left an orphan when I was a little shaver, knee-high to a toadstool. Uncle Dick, he took me home. Aunt Marthy didn't like it, I guess. All she said was, ' Massy me! another mouth to feed?' ' Pooh, pooh, Marthy,' uncle laughed, ' where there's enough for two, there's enough for three.' She shut up, but she never liked me one mite."

" An orphan?" interjected Charley. " No father nor mother?"

" I'll tell you about it. You see, my father went out mate on a whaling voyage in the Pacific, in this very same old *Argonaut* we've been patchin' and pluggin' up. It may have been a year we got a letter telling he was dead. Boat he was in swamped, while fast to a whale—a big one. They picked up his hat. Sharks took him, I guess. Mother was poorly. She fell into a decline, they called it, and didn't live long. We had nothin' but father's wages. They was only a drop in the bucket. Then there was only me left."

" That was the time your uncle took you home? "

" Yes; Uncle Dick was a rigger by trade. He used to show me how to make all sorts of knots and splices evenings; and bimeby he got me a chance, when I was big enough, doin' odd jobs like, for a dollar a week, in the loft or on the ships. Aunt Marthy said a dollar a week didn't begin to pay for what I et. Guess she knew. Pretty soon, I got a raise to a dollar-half."

" But what made you quit? Didn't you like the work? "

" Liked it first-rate. Like it now. But I

couldn't stand Aunt Marthy's sour looks and sharp tongue. Nothing suited her. She was either as cold as ice, or as hot as fire coals. When she wasn't scolding, she was groaning. Said she couldn't see what some folks was born into this world just to slave for other folks for." A frown passed over Walter's face at the recollection.

"Nice woman that," observed the sententious Charley. "But how about the uncle?" he added. "Couldn't he make her hold her yawp?"

"Oh, no better man ever stood. He was like a father to me—bless him!" (Walter's voice grew a little shaky here.) "But he showed the white feather to Aunt Marthy. Whenever she went into one of her tantrums, he would take his pipe and clear out, leaving me to bear the brunt of it.

"A good while after mother died, father's sea-chest was brought home in the *Argonaut*. There was nothing in it but old clothes, this watch [showing it], and some torn and greasy sea-charts, with the courses father had sailed pricked out on 'em. Those charts made me sort o' hanker to see the world, which I then saw men traveled with the aid of a roll of paper, and a little knowledge, as certainly, and as safely, as we do the streets of Boston. You better believe I studied over those charts some! Anyhow, I know my geography." And Walter's blue eyes lighted up with a look of triumph.

"Bully for you! Then that was what started you out on your travels, was it?"

"No: I had often thought of slipping away some dark night, but couldn't make up my mind to it. It did seem so kind o' mean after all Uncle Dick had done for me. But one day (one bad day for me, Charley) a man came running up to the loft, all out of breath, to tell me that Uncle Dick had fallen down the ship's hatchway, and that they were now bringing him home on a stretcher. I tell you I felt sick and faint when I saw him lying there lifeless. He never spoke again.

" Shortly after the funeral, upon going to the loft the foreman told me that work being slack they would have to lay off a lot of hands, me with the rest.   Before I went to sleep that night I made up my mind to strike out for myself; for now that Uncle Dick was gone, I couldn't endure my life any longer.   I set about packing up my duds without saying anything to my aunt, for I knew what a rumpus she would make over it, and if there's anything I hate it's a scene."

" Me too," Charley vigorously assented. " Rather take a lickin'."

" Well," Walter resumed, " I counted up my money first.   There was just forty-nine dollars.   Lucky number: it was the year '49 too.   I put ten of it in an envelope directed to my aunt, and put it on the chimney-piece where she couldn't help seeing it when she came into my room.   Then I took a piece of chalk and wrote on the table top: ' I'm going away to hunt for work.   When I get some, I'll let you know.   Please take care of my

chest.   Look on the mantelpiece.   Good-bye.
From Walter.'

"Then, like a thief, I slipped out of the
house by a back way, in my stocking feet, and
never stopped running till I was 'way out of
town.   There I struck the railroad.   I knew
if I followed it it would take me to Boston.
And it did.   That's all."

III

AND CHARLEY TELLS HIS

THERE was silence for a minute or two, each of the lads being busy with his own thoughts. Apparently they were not pleasant thoughts. What a tantalizing thing memory sometimes is!

But it was not in the nature of things for either to remain long speechless. Walter first broke silence by reminding Charley of his promise. "Come now, you've wormed all that out of me about my folks, pay your debts. I should like to know what made you leave home. Did you run away, too?"

At this question, Charley's mouth puckered up queerly, and then quickly broke out into a broad grin, while his eyes almost shut tight at the recollection Walter's question had summoned up. " It was all along of ' Rough on Rats,' " he managed to say at last.

" ' Rough on Rats? ' "

" Yes, ' Rough on Rats.' Rat poison. You just wait, and hear me through.

" I've got a father somewhere, I b'leeve. Boys gen'ally have, I s'pose, though whether mine's dead or alive, not knowin', can't say. We were poor as Job's turkey, if you know how poor that was. I don't. Anyway, he put me out to work on a milk and chicken farm back here in the country, twenty miles or so, to a man by the name of Bennett, and then took himself off out West somewhere."

" And you've never seen him since? "

" No; I ha'n't never missed him, or the lickin's he give me. Well, my boss he raised lots of young chickens for market. We was awfully pestered with rats, big, fat, sassy ones, getting into the coops nights, and killing off the little chicks as soon's ever they was hatched out. You see, they was tender. Besides eating the chicks they et up most of the grain we throw'd into the hens. The boss he tried everything to drive those rats away. He tried cats an' he tried traps. 'Twan't no use. The cats wouldn't tech the rats nor the rats go near the traps. You can't fool an old rat much, anyhow," he added with a knowing shake of his head.

"Well, the boss was a-countin' the chicks one mornin', while ladling out the dough to 'em. 'Confound those rats,' he sputtered out; 'there's eight more chicks gone sence I fed last night. I'd gin something to red the place on 'em, I would.'

"'Uncle,' says I (he let me call him uncle, seein' he'd kind of adopted me like) — 'uncle,' says I, 'why don't you try Rough on Rats? They say that 'll fetch 'em every time.'

"'What's that? Never heer'd on't. How do you know? Who says so?' he axed all in one breath."

"'Anyhow, I seen a big poster down at the Four Corners that says so,' says I. 'The boys was a-talkin' about what it had done up to Skillings' place. Skillings allowed he'd red his place of rats with it. Hadn't seen hide nor hair of one sence he fust tried it. Everybody says it's a big thing.'

" The old man said nothin' more just then. He didn't let on that my advice was worth a cent; but I noticed that he went off and bought some Rough on Rats that same afternoon, and when the old hens had gone to roost and the mother hens had gathered their broods under 'em for the night, uncle he slyly stirred up a big dose of the p'isen stuff into a pan of meal, which he set down inside the henhouse.

" Uncle's idea was to get up early in the mornin', so's to count up the dead rats, I s'pose.

" But he did not get up early enough. When he went out into the henhouse to investigate, he found fifteen or twenty of his best hens lying dead around the floor after eatin' of the p'isen'd meal.

" When I come outdoors he was stoopin'

down, with his back to me pickin' 'em up."

Walter laughed until the tears rolled down his cheeks, sobered down, and then broke out again.   Charley found the laugh infectious and joined in it, though more moderately.

"Go ahead.   Let's have the rest, do," Walter entreated.   "What next?"

"I asked Uncle Bennett what he was goin' to do with all those dead hens.   He flung one at my head.   Oh! but he was mad.   'Just stop where you be, my little joker,' says he, startin' off for the stable; 'I've got somethin' that's Rough on Brats, an' you shall have a taste on't right off.   Don't you stir a step,' shakin' his fist at me, ' or I'll give you the worst dressin' down you ever had in all your life.'

"While he was gone for a horsewhip, I lit out for the Corners.   You couldn't have seen me for dust.

"I darsen't go back to the house and I had only a silver ninepence in my pocket and a few coppers, but I managed to beg my way to Boston. Oh! Walt, it was a long time between meals, I can tell you. I slept one night in a barn, on the haymow. Nobody saw me slip in after dark. I took off my neckerchief and laid it down within reach, for it was hot weather on that haymow, and I was 'most choked with the dust I swallowed. I overslept. In the morning I heard a noise down where the hosses were tied up. Some one was rakin' down hay for 'em. I reached for my neckerchief, thinkin' how I should get away without being seen, when a boy's voice gave a shout, 'Towser! Towser!' and then I knew it was all up, for that boy had raked down my neckerchief with the hay, and he knew there was a tramp somewhere about.

"The long and short of it is, that the dog chased me till I was ready to drop or until another and a bigger one came out of a yard and tackled him. Then it was dog eat dog.

"When I got to Boston it was night. I had no money. I didn't know where to go.

Tired's no name for it. I was dead-beat.
So I threw myself down on a doorstep and
was asleep in a minnit.   There was an alarm
of fire.   An ingine came jolting along.   I
forgot all about being tired and took holt of
the rope, and ran, and hollered, with the rest.
The fire was all out when we got there, so I
went back to the ingine house, and the stew-
ard let me sleep in the cellar a couple of hours
and wash up in the mornin'.   But I'm ahead
of my story.   They had hot coffee and crack-
ers and cheese when they got back from the
fire.   No cheese ever tasted like that before.
Give me a fireman for a friend at need.   I
hung round that ingine house till I picked up
a job.   The company was all calkers, grav-
ers, riggers, and the like.   Tough lot !   How
they could wallop that old tub over the cobble-
stones, to be sure ! "

And here Charley fell into a fit of musing
from which Walter did not attempt to rouse
him.   In their past experiences the two boys
had found a common bond.

IV

SEEING that Walter also had fallen into a brown study, Charley quickly changed the subject. " See here, Walt ! " he exclaimed, " the *Argonaut's* going to sail for Californy first fair wind. To-morrow's Sunday, and Father Taylor's goin' to preach aboard of her. He's immense ! Let's go and hear him. What do you say ? "

Walter jumped at the proposal. " I want to hear Father Taylor ever so much, and I shouldn't mind taking a look at the passengers, too."

Sunday came. Walter put on his best suit, and the two friends strolled down to the wharf where the *Argonaut* lay moored with topsails loosened, and flags and streamers flut-

tering gayly aloft.   The ship was thronged
not only with those about to sail for the Land
of Gold, but also with the friends who had
come to bid them good-bye; besides many attracted by mere curiosity, or, perhaps, by the
fame of Father Taylor's preaching.   There
was a perfect Babel of voices.   As Walter
was passing one group he overheard the remark, "She'll never get round the Horn.
Too deep.   Too many passengers by half.
Look at that bow!   Have to walk round her
to tell stem from starn."

"Oh, she'll get there fast enough," his
companion replied.   "She knows the way.
Besides, you can't sink her.   She's got lumber
enough in her hold to keep her afloat if she
should get waterlogged."

"That ain't the whole story by a long
shot," a third speaker broke in.   "Don't you
remember the crack ship that spoke an old
whaler at sea, both bound out for California?
The passengers on the crack ship called out to
the passengers on the old whaler to know if

they wanted to be reported. When the crack ship got into San Francisco, lo and behold! there lay the ' old tub ' quietly at anchor. Been in a week."

Strange sight, indeed, it was to see men who, but the day before, were clerks in sober tweeds, farmers in homespun, or mechanics in greasy overalls, now so dressed up as to look far more like brigands than peaceful citizens; for it would seem that, to their notion, they could be no true Californians unless they started off armed to the teeth. So the poor stay-at-homes were given to understand how wanting they were in the bold spirit of adventure by a lavish display of pistols and bowie-knives, rifles and carbines. Poor creatures! they little knew how soon they were to meet an enemy not to be overcome with powder and lead.

Between decks, if the truth must be told, many of the passengers were engaged in sparring or wrestling bouts, playing cards, or shuffleboard, or hop-scotch, as regardless of the day as if going to California meant a cutting loose from all the restraints of civilized life. The two friends made haste to get on deck. As they mingled with the crowd again, Walter exchanged quick glances with a middle-aged gentleman on whose arm a remarkably pretty young lady was leaning. Walter was saying to himself, " I wonder where I have seen that man before," when the full and sonorous voice of Father Taylor, the seaman's friend, hushed the confused murmur of voices around him into a reverential silence. With none of the arts and graces of the pulpit orator, that short, thick-set, hardfeatured man spoke like one inspired for a full hour, and during that hour nobody stirred from the spot where he had taken his stand. Father Taylor's every word had struck home.

The last hymn had been sung, the last prayer said. At its ending the crowd slowly began filing down the one long, narrow plank reaching from the ship's gangway to the wharf. Nobody seemed to have noticed that the rising tide had lifted this plank to an incline that would make the descent trying to weak nerves, especially as there were five or six feet of clear water to be passed over between ship and shore. It was just as one young lady was in the act of stepping upon this plank that two young scapegraces ahead of her ran down it with such violence as to make it rebound like a springboard, causing the young lady first to lose her balance, then to make a false step, and then to fall screaming into the water, twenty feet below.

Everybody ran to that side, and everybody began shouting at once: " Man overboard ! " " A boat: get a boat ! " " Throw over a rope ! —a plank ! " " She's going down ! " " Help ! help !" but nobody seemed to have their wits about them. With the hundreds looking on, it really seemed as if the girl might drown before help could reach her.

Both Charley and Walter had witnessed the accident: coats and hats were off in a jiffy. Snatching up a coil of rope, it was the work of a moment for Walter to make a running noose, slip that under his arms, sign to Charley to take a turn round a bitt, then to swing himself over into the chains and be lowered down into the water on the run by the quick-witted Charley.

Meantime, the young lady's father was almost beside himself. In one breath he called to his daughter, by the name of Dora, to catch at a rope that was too short to reach her; in the next he was offering fifty, a hundred dollars to Walter if he saved her.

Giving himself a vigorous shove with his foot, in two or three strokes Walter was at the girl's side and with his arms around her. It was high time, too, as her clothes, which had buoyed her up so far, were now water-soaked and dragging her down. Only her head was to be seen above water. At Walter's cheery " Haul away! " fifty nervous arms dragged them dripping up the ship's side. The young lady fell, sobbing hysterically, into her father's arms, and was forthwith hurried off into the

Walter rescuing Dora Bright. — *Page 42.*

cabin, while Walter, after picking up his coat
and hat, slipped off through the crowd, gained
the wharf unnoticed, and with the faithful,
but astonished, Charley at his heels, made a
bee-line for his lodgings. Moreover, Walter exacted a solemn promise from Charley
not to lisp one word of what had happened,
on pain of a good drubbing.

" My best suit, too ! " he ruefully exclaimed,
while divesting himself of his wet clothes.
" No matter : let him keep his old fifty dollars. Pretty girl, though. I'm paid ten
times over. A coil of rope's a handy thing
sometimes. So's a rigger—eh, Charley?"

Charley merely gave a dissatisfied grunt.
He was very far from understanding such
refined sentiments. Besides, half the money,
he reflected, would have been his, or ought to
have been, which was much the same thing to
his way of thinking. And when he thought
of the many things he could have done with
his share, the loss of it made him feel very
miserable, and more than half angry with

Walter. " Fifty dollars don't grow on every bush," he muttered. " Then, what lions we'd 'a' been in the papers!" he lamented.

" You look here. Can't you do anything without being paid for it? I'd taken thanks from the old duffer, but not money. Can't you understand? Now you keep still about this, I tell you."

Though still grumbling, Charley concluded to hold his tongue, knowing that Walter would be as good as his word; but he inwardly promised himself to keep his eyes open, and if ever he should see a chance to let the cat out of the bag without Walter's knowing it, well, the mischief was in it if he, Charley, didn't improve it, that was all.

V

ONE WAY OF GOING TO CALIFORNIA

THE *Argonaut* affair got into the newspapers, where it was correctly reported, in the main, except that the rescuer was supposed to be one of the *Argonaut's* passengers, and as she was now many miles at sea, Mr. Bright, the father of Dora, as a last resort, put an advertisement in the daily papers asking the unknown to furnish his address without delay to his grateful debtors. But as this failed to elicit a reply, there was nothing more to be done.

Walter, however, had seen the advertisement, and he had found out from it that Mr. Bright was one of the *Argonaut's* principal owners. He therefore felt quite safe from discovery when he found himself reported as having sailed in that vessel.

Time moved along quietly enough with Walter until the Fourth of July was near at hand, when it began to be noised about that the brand-new clipper ship then receiving her finishing touches in a neighboring yard would be launched at high water on that eventful day. What was unusual, the nameless ship was to be launched fully rigged, so that the riggers' gang was to take a hand in getting her off the ways. Everybody was consequently on the tiptoe of expectation.

The eventful morning came at last. It being a holiday, thousands had repaired to the spot, attracted by the novelty of seeing a ship launched fully rigged. At a given signal, a hundred sledges, wielded by as many brawny arms, began a furious hammering away at the blocks, which held the gallant ship bound and helpless to the land. The men worked like tigers, as if each and every one had a personal interest in the success of the launch. At last the clatter of busy hammers ceased, the grimy workmen crept out, in twos and threes, from underneath the huge black hull, and a hush fell upon all that vast throng, so deep and breathless that the streamers at the mast-head could be heard snapping like so many whiplashes in the light breeze aloft.

" All clear for'ard? " sang out the master workman. " All clear, sir," came back the quick response. " All clear aft? " the voice repeated. " Aye, aye, all clear." Still the towering mass did not budge. It really seemed as if she was a living creature hesitating on the brink of her own fate, whether to make the plunge or not. There was an anxious moment. A hush fell upon all that vast throng. Then, as the stately ship was seen to move majestically off, first slowly, and then with a rush and a leap, one deafening shout went up from a thousand throats: " There she goes! there she goes! hurrah! hurrah! " Every one declared it the prettiest launch ever seen.

Just as the nameless vessel glided off the ways a young lady, who stood upon a tall scaffold at the bow, quickly dashed a bottle of wine against the stem, pronouncing as she did so the name that the good ship was to bear henceforth, so proudly, on the seas—the *Flying Arrow*. Three rousing cheers greeted the act, and the name. The crowd then began to disperse.

As Walter was standing quite near the platform erected for this ceremony, his face all aglow with the vigorous use he had made of the sledge he still held in his hand, the young lady who had just christened the *Flying Arrow* came down the stairs. In doing so, she looked Master Walter squarely in the face. Lo and behold! it was the girl of the *Argonaut*. The recognition was instant and mutual.

Walter turned all colors at once. Giving one glance at his greasy duck trousers and checked shirt, his first impulse was to sneak off without a word; but before he could do so he was confronted by Mr. Bright himself. Walter was thus caught, as it were, between two fires. Oh, brave youth of the stalwart arm and manly brow, thus to show the white feather to that weak and timid little maiden!

Noticing the young man's embarrassment, Mr. Bright drew him aside, out of earshot of those who still lingered about. "So, so, my young friend," he began with a quizzical look at Walter, "we've had some trouble finding you. Pray what were your reasons for avoiding us? Neither of us [turning toward his daughter] is a very dangerous person, as you may see for yourself."

"Now, don't, papa," pleaded Dora. Then, after giving a sidelong and reproachful look at Walter, she added, "Why, he wouldn't even let us thank him!"

Walter tried to stammer out something about not deserving thanks. The words seemed to stick in his throat; but he did manage to say: "Fifty stood ready to do what I did. I only got a little wetting, sir."

"Just so. But they didn't, all the same.

Come, we are not ungrateful. Can I depend on you to call at my office, 76 State Street, to-morrow morning about ten?"

"You can, sir," bowing respectfully.

"Very good. I shall expect you. Come, Dora, we must be going." Father and daughter then left the yard, but not until Dora had given Walter another reproachful look, out of the corner of her eye.

"Poor, proud, and sheepish," was the merchant's only comment upon this interview, as they walked homeward. Mentally, he was asking himself where he had seen that face before.

Dora said nothing. Her stolen glances had told her, however, that Walter was good-looking; and that was much in his favor. To be sure, he was plainly a common workman, and he had appeared very stiff and awkward when her father spoke to him. Still she felt that there was nothing low or vulgar about him.

Punctual to the minute, Walter entered

the merchant's counting room, though, to say truth, he found himself ill at ease in the presence of half a dozen spruce-looking clerks, who first shot sly glances at him, then at each other, as he carefully shut the door behind him. Walter, however, bore their scrutiny without flinching. He was only afraid of girls, from sixteen to eighteen years old.

Mr. Bright immediately rose from his desk, and beckoned Walter to follow him out into the warehouse. " You are prompt. That's well," said he approvingly. " Now then, to business. We want an outdoor clerk on our wharf. You have no objection, I take it, to entering our employment? "

Walter shook his head. " Oh, no, sir."

" Very good, then. I'll tell you more of your duties presently. I hear a good account of you. The salary will be six hundred the first year, and a new suit of clothes, in return for the one you spoiled. Here's a tailor's address [handing Walter a card with the order written upon it]. Go and get measured when you like, and mind you get a good fit."

Walter took a moment to think, but couldn't think at all. All he could say was: " If you think, sir, I can fill the place, I'll try my best to suit you."

" That's right. Try never was beat. You may begin to-morrow." Walter went off feeling more happy than he remembered ever to have felt before.   In truth, he could hardy realize his good fortune.

This change in Walter's life brought with it other changes.   For one thing it broke off his intimacy with Charley, although Walter continued to receive occasional visits from his old chum. He also began attending an evening school, kept by a retired schoolmaster, in order to improve his knowledge of writing, spelling, and arithmetic, or rather to repair the neglect of years; for he now began to feel his deficiencies keenly with increasing responsibilities.   He was, however, an apt scholar, and was soon making good progress.   The work on the wharf was far more to his liking than the confinement of the warehouse could have been; and Walter was every day storing up information which some time, he believed, would be of great use to him.

Time wore on, one day's round being much like another's. But once Walter was given such a fright that he did not get over it for weeks. He was sometimes sent to the bank to make a deposit or cash a check. On this particular occasion he had drawn out quite a large sum, in small bills, to be used in paying off the help. Not knowing what else to do with it, Walter thrust the roll of bills into his trousers pocket. It was raining gently out of doors, and the sidewalks were thickly spread with a coating of greasy mud. There was another call or two to be made before Walter returned to the store. At the head of the street Walter stopped to think which call he should make first. Mechanically he thrust his hand in his pocket, then turned as pale as a sheet, and a mist passed before his eyes.

The roll of bills was not there. A hole in the pocket told the whole story. The roll had slipped out somewhere. It was gone, and through his own carelessness.

After a moment's indecision Walter started back to the bank, carefully looking for the lost roll at every step of the way. The street was full of people, for this was the busiest hour of the day. In vain he looked, and looked, at every one he met. No one had a roll of bills for which he was trying to find an owner. Almost beside himself, he rushed into the bank. Yes, the paying teller remembered him, but was quite sure the lost roll had not been picked up there, or he would have known it. So Walter's last and faintest hope now vanished. Go back to the office with his strange story, he dared not. The bank teller advised his reporting his loss to the police, and advertising it in the evening editions. Slowly and sadly Walter retraced his steps towards the spot where he had first missed his employer's money, inwardly scolding and accusing himself by turns. Vexed beyond measure, calling himself all the fools he could think of, Walter angrily stamped his foot on the sidewalk. Presto! out tumbled the missing roll of bills from the bottom of his trousers-leg when he brought his foot down with such force. It had been caught and held there by the stiffening material then fashionable.

Walter went home that night thanking his lucky stars that he had come out of a bad scrape so easily. He was thinking over the matter, when Charley burst into the room. " I say, Walt, old fel, don't you want to buy a piece of me?" he blurted out, tossing his cap on the table, and falling into a chair quite out of breath.

Walter simply stared, and for a minute the two friends stared at each other without speaking. Walter at length demanded: " Are you crazy, Charles Wormwood? What in the name of common sense do you mean? "

"Oh, I'm not fooling. You needn't be scared. Haven't you ever heard of folks buying pieces of ships? Say?"

"S'pose I have; what's that got to do with men?"

"I'll tell you. Look here. When a feller wants to go to Californy awful bad, like me, and hasn't got the chink, like me, he gets some other fellers who can't go, like you, to chip in to pay his passage for him."

"Pooh! That's all plain sailing. When he earns the money he pays it back," Walter rejoined.

"No, you're all out. Just you hold your hosses. It's like this. The chap who gets the send-off binds himself, good and strong, mind you, to divide what he makes out there among his owners, 'cordin' to what they put into him—same's owning pieces of a ship, ain't it? See? How big a piece 'll you take?" finished Charley, cracking his knuckles in his impatience.

Walter leaned back in his chair, and burst

out in a fit of uncontrollable laughter. Charley grew red in the face. " Look here, Walt, you needn't have any if you don't want it." He took up his cap to go. Walter stopped him.

" There, you needn't get your back up, old chap. It's the funniest thing I ever heard of. Why, it beats all! "

" It's done every day," Charley broke in. " You won't lose anything by me, Walt," he added, anxiously scanning Walter's face. " See if you do."

Walter had saved a little money. He therefore agreed to become a shareholder in Charles Wormwood, Esquire, to the tune of fifty dollars, said Wormwood duly agreeing and covenanting, on his part, to pay over dividends as fast as earned. So the ingenious Charley sailed with as good a kit as could be picked up in Boston, not omitting a beautiful Colt's revolver (Walter's gift), on which was engraved, " Use me; don't abuse me." Charles was to work his passage out in the

new clipper, which arrangement would land
him in San Francisco with his capital unim-
paired. " God bless you, Charley, my boy,"
stammered Walter, as the two friends wrung
each other's hands. He could not have
spoken another word without breaking down,
which would have been positive degradation
in a boy's eyes.

" I'll make your fortune, see if I don't,"
was Charley's cheerful farewell. " On the
square I will," he brokenly added.

The house of Bright, Wantage & Company
had a confidential clerk for whom Walter felt
a secret antipathy from the first day they met.
We cannot explain these things; we only know
that they exist. It may be a senseless preju-
dice; no matter, we cannot help it. This
clerk's name was Ramon Ingersoll. His manner toward his fellow clerks was so top-lofty
and so condescending that one and all thoroughly disliked him. Some slight claim Ramon was supposed to have upon the senior
partner, Mr. Bright, kept the junior clerks

somewhat in awe of him. But there was always friction in the counting-room when the clerks were left alone together.

The truth is that Ramon's father had at one time acted as agent for the house at Matanzas, in Cuba. When he died, leaving nothing but debts and this one orphan child, for he had buried his wife some years before, Mr. Bright had taken the little Ramon home, sent him to school, paid all his expenses out of his own pocket and finally given him a place of trust in his counting-house. In a word, this orphaned, penniless boy owed everything to his benefactor.

As has been already mentioned, without being able to give a reason for his belief, Walter had an instinctive feeling that Ramon would some day get him into trouble. Fortunately Walter's duties kept him mostly outside the warehouse, so that the two seldom met.

One day Ramon, with more than ordinary cordiality, asked Walter to visit him at his

room that same evening in order to meet, as
he said, one or two particular friends of his.
At the appointed time Walter went, without
mistrust, to Ingersoll's lodgings. Upon entering the room he found there two very
flashy-looking men, one of whom was short,
fat, and smooth-shaven, with an oily good-
natured leer lurking about the corners of his
mouth; the other dark-browed, bearded, and
scowling, with, as Walter thought, as desperately villainous a face as he had ever looked
upon.

"Ah, here you are, at last!" cried Ramon,
as he let Walter in. "This is Mr. Goodman," here the fat man bowed, and smiled
blandly; "and this, Mr. Lambkin." The
dark man looked up, scowled, and nodded.
"And now," Ramon went on, "as we have
been waiting for you, what say you to a little
game of whist, or high-low-jack, or euchre,
just to pass away the time?"

"I'm agreeable," said Mr. Goodman,
"though, upon my word and honor, I hardly

know one card from another. However, just
to make up your party, I will take a hand."

The knight of the gloomy brow silently
drew his chair up to the table, which was, at
least, significant of his intentions.

Walter had no scruples about playing an
innocent game of whist. So he sat down with
the others.

The game went on rather languidly until,
all at once, the fat man broke out, without
taking his eyes off his cards, " Bless me!—
why, the strangest thing!—if I were a betting
man, I declare I wouldn't mind risking a trifle
on this hand."

Ramon laughed good-naturedly, as he replied in an offhand sort of way: " Oh, we're
all friends here. There's no objection to a
little social game, I suppose, among friends."
Here he stole an inquiring look at Walter.
" Besides," he continued, while carelessly
glancing at his own hand, " I've a good mind
to bet a trifle myself."

Though still quite unsuspicious, Walter

looked upon this interruption of the harmless game with misgiving.

"All right," Goodman resumed, "here goes a dollar, just for the fun of the thing."

The taciturn Lambkin said not a word, but taking out a well-stuffed wallet, quietly laid down two dollars on the one that Goodman had just put up.

"I know I can beat them," Ramon whispered in Walter's ear. "By Jove, I'll risk it just this once!"

"No, don't," Walter whispered back, pleadingly, "it's gambling."

"Pshaw, man, it's only for sport," Ramon impatiently rejoined, immediately adding five dollars of his own money to the three before him.

Walter laid down his cards, leaned back in his chair, and folded his arms resolutely across his chest. "And the fat man said he hardly knew one card from another. How quick some folks do learn," he said to himself.

" Isn't our young friend going to try his luck? " smiled, rather than asked, the unctuous Goodman.

" No; I never play for money," was the quiet response.

Once the ice was broken the game went on for higher, and still higher, stakes, until Walter, getting actually frightened at the recklessness with which Ramon played and lost, rose to go.

After vainly urging him to remain, annoyed at his failure to make Walter play, enraged by his own losses, Ramon followed Walter outside the door, shut it behind them, and said in a menacing sort of way, " Not a word of this at the store."

" Promise you won't play any more."

" I won't do no such thing. Who set you up for my guardian? If you're mean enough to play the sneak, tell if you dare! "

Walter felt his anger rising, but controlled himself. " Oh, very well, only remember that I warned you," he replied, turning away.

"Don't preach, Master Innocence!" sneered Ramon.

"Don't threaten, Master Hypocrite!" was the angry retort.

Quick as a flash, Ramon sprang before Walter, and barred his way. All the tiger in his nature gleamed in his eyes. "One word of this to Mr. Bright, and I'll—I'll fix you!" he almost shrieked out.

With that the two young men clinched, and for a few minutes nothing could be heard but their heavy breathing. This did not last. Walter soon showed himself much the stronger of the two, and Master Ramon, in spite of his struggles, found himself lying flat on his back, with his adversary's knee on his chest. Ramon instantly gave in. Choking down his wrath, he jerked out, "There, I promise. Let me up."

"Oh, if you promise, so do I," said Walter, releasing his hold on Ramon. He then left the house without another word. He did not see Ramon shaking his fist behind his back, or hear him muttering threats of vengeance to himself, as he went back to his vicious companions. Walter did wish, however, that he had given Ramon just one more punch for keeps.

So they parted. Satisfied that Walter would not break his promise, Ramon made all haste back to his companions, laughing in his sleeve to think how easily he had fooled that milksop Seabury. His companions were two as notorious sharpers as Boston contained. He continued to lose heavily, they luring him on by letting him win now and then, until they were satisfied he had nothing more to lose. At two in the morning their victim rose up from the table, hardly realizing, so far gone was he in liquor, that he was five hundred dollars in debt to Lambkin, or that he had signed a note for that sum with the name of his employers, Bright, Wantage & Company. He had found the road from gambling to forgery a natural and easy one.

VI

A BLACK SHEEP IN THE FOLD

LEAVING Ingersoll to follow his crooked ways, we must now introduce a character, with whom Walter had formed an acquaintance, destined to have no small influence upon his own future life.

Bill Portlock was probably as good a specimen of an old, battered man-o'-war's man as could be scared up between Montauk and Quoddy Head. While a powder-monkey, on board the *President* frigate, he had been taken prisoner and confined in Dartmoor Prison, from which he had made his escape, with some companions in captivity, by digging a hole under the foundation wall with an old iron spoon. Shipping on board a British merchantman, he had deserted at the first neutral port she touched at. He was now doing

odd jobs about the wharves, as 'longshore-
man; and as Walter had thrown many such
in the old salt's way a kind of intimacy had
grown up between them. Bill loved dearly
to spin a yarn, and some of his adventures,
told in his own vernacular, would have made
the late Baron Munchausen turn green with
envy. " Why," he would say, after spinning
one of his wonderful yarns, " ef I sh'd tell ye
my adventers, man and boy, you'd think
'twas Roberson Crushoe a-talkin' to ye. No
need o' lyin'. Sober airnest beats all they
make up."

Bill's castle was a condemned caboose, left
on the wharf by some ship that was now plow-
ing some distant sea. Her name, the *Orpheus,* could still be read in faded paint on the
caboose; so that Bill always claimed to belong to the *Orpheus,* or she to him, he couldn't
exactly say which. When he was at work on
the wharf, after securing his castle with a
stout padlock, he announced the fact to an inquiring public by chalking up the legend,

"Aboard the brig," or "Aboard the skoner," as the case might be. If called to take a passenger off to some vessel in his wherry, the notice would then read, "Back at eight bells." A sailor he was, and a sailor he said he would live and die.

No one but a sailor, and an old sailor at that, could have squeezed himself into the narrow limits of the caboose, where it was not possible, even for a short man like Bill, to stand upright, though Bill himself considered it quite luxurious living. There was a rusty old cooking stove at one end, with two legs of its own, and two replaced by half-bricks; the other end being taken up by a bench, from which Bill deftly manipulated saucepan or skillet.

"Why, Lor' bless ye!" said Bill to Walter one evening, "I seed ye fish that ar' young 'ooman out o' the dock that time. 'Bill,' sez I to myself, 'thar's a chap, now, as knows a backstay from a bullock's tail.'"

"Pshaw!" Then after a moment's silence, while Bill was busy lighting his pipe, Walter absently asked, " Bill, were you ever in California? "

" Kalerforny? Was I ever in Kalerforny? Didn't I go out to Sandy Ager, in thirty-eight, in a hide drogher? And d'ye know why they call it Sandy Ager? I does. Why, blow me if it ain't sandy 'nuff for old Cape Cod herself; and as for the ager, if you'll b'leeve me, our ship's crew shook so with it, that all hands had to turn to a-settin' up rig-gin' twict a month, it got so slack with the shakin' up like."

" What an unhealthy place that must be," laughed Walter. Then suddenly changing the subject, he said: " Bill, you know the *Racehorse* is a good two months overdue." Bill nodded. " I know our folks are getting uneasy about her. No wonder. Valuable cargo, and no insurance. What's your idea? "

Bill gave a few whiffs at his pipe before replying. " I know that ar' *Racehorse.*

She's a clipper, and has a good sailor aboard of her: but heavy sparred, an' not the kind to be carryin' sail on in the typhoon season, jest to make a quick passage." Bill shook his head. "Like as not she's dismasted, or sprung a leak, an' the Lord knows what all."

The next day happened to be Saturday. As Walter was going into the warehouse he met Ramon coming out. Since the night at his lodgings, his manner toward Walter, outwardly at least, had undergone a marked change. If anything it was too cordial. "Hello! Seabury, that you?" he said, in his offhand way. "Lucky thing you happened in. It's steamer day, and I'm awfully hard pushed for time. Would you mind getting this check on the Suffolk cashed for me? No? That's a good fellow. Do as much for you some time. And, stay, on your way back call at the California steamship agency —you know?—all right. Well, see if there are any berths left in the *Georgia*. You won't forget the name? The *Georgia*. And, oh! be sure to get gold for that check. It's to pay duties with, you know," Ramon hurriedly explained in an undertone.

"All right; I understand," said Walter, walking briskly away on his errand. He quite forgot all about the gold, though, until after he had left the bank; when, suddenly remembering it, he hurried back to get the coin, quite flurried and provoked at his own forgetfulness. The cashier, however, counted out the double-eagles, for the notes, without remark. Such little instances of forgetfulness were too common to excite his particular notice.

On that same evening, finding time hanging rather heavily on his hands, Walter strolled uptown in the direction of Mr. Bright's house, which was in the fashionable Mt. Vernon Street. The truth is that the silly boy thought he might possibly catch a glimpse of a certain young lady, or her shadow, at least, in passing the brilliantly lighted residence. It was, he admitted to

himself, a fool's errand, after walking slowly
backwards and forwards two or three times,
with his eyes fastened upon the lighted windows; and with a feeling of disappointment he
turned away from the spot, heartily ashamed
of himself, as well, for having given way to
a sudden impulse.   Glad he was that no one
had noticed him.

Walter's queer actions, however, did not
escape the attention of a certain lynx-eyed
policeman, who, snugly ensconced in the
shadow of a doorway, had watched his every
step.   The young man had gone but a short
distance on his homeward way, when, as he
was about crossing the street, he came within
an ace of being knocked down and run over
by a passing hack, which turned the corner at
such a break-neck pace that there was barely
time to get out of the way.   There was a gas-
light on this corner.   At Walter's warning
shout to the driver, the person inside the hack
quickly put his head out of the window, and
as quickly drew it in again; but in that instant

the light had shone full upon the face of Ramon Ingersoll.

The driver lashed his horses into a run. Walter stood stupidly staring after the carriage. Then, without knowing why, he ran after it, confident that if he had recognized Ramon in that brief moment, Ramon must also have recognized him. The best he could do, however, was to keep the carriage in sight, but he soon saw that it was heading for the railway station at the South End.

Out of breath, and nearly out of his head, too, Walter dashed through the arched doorway of the station, just in time to see a train going out at the other end in a cloud of smoke. In his eagerness, Walter ran headlong into the arms of the night-watchman, who, seeing the blank look on Walter's face, said, as he had said a hundred times before to belated travelers, " Too late, eh? "

" Yes, yes, too late," repeated Walter, in a tone of deep vexation. While walking home he began to think he had been making a fool of himself again.   After all, what business was it of his if Ramon had gone to New York?   He might have gone on business of the firm.   Of course that was it.   And what right had he, Walter, to be chasing Ramon through the streets, anyhow?   Still, he was sure that Ramon had recognized him, and just as sure that Ramon had wished to avoid being recognized, else why had he not spoken or even waved his hand?   Walter gave it up, and went home to dream of chasing carriages all night long.

Walter went to the wharf as usual the next morning.   In the course of the forenoon a porter brought word that he was wanted at the counting-room.   When Walter went into the office, Mr. Bright was walking the floor, back and forth, with hasty steps, while a very dark, clean-shaven, alert-looking man sat leaning back in a chair before the door.   This person immediately arose, locked the office door, put the key in his pocket, and then quietly sat down again.

Walter's heart was in his mouth. He grew red and pale by turns. Before he could collect his ideas Mr. Bright stopped in his walk, looked him squarely in the eye, and, in an altered voice, demanded sharply and sternly: "Ingersoll—where is he? No prevarication. I want the truth and nothing but the truth. You understand?"

Walter tried hard to make a composed answer, but the words would not seem to come; and the merchant's cold gray eyes seemed searching him through and through. However, he managed to stammer out: "I don't know, sir, where he is—gone away, hasn't he?"

"Don't know. Gone away," repeated the merchant. "Now answer me directly, without any ifs or buts; where, and when, did you see him last?"

"Last night; at least, I thought it was Ramon." The dark man gave his head a little toss.

"Well, go on? What then?"

" It was about nine o'clock, in a close carriage, not far from the Common." That, by the way, was as near to Mr. Bright's house as Walter thought proper to locate the affair.

Mr. Bright exchanged glances with the dark man, who merely nodded, but said never a word.

Thinking his examination was over, Walter plucked up the courage to say of his own accord, " I ran after the carriage as tight as I could; but you see, sir, the driver was lashing his horses all the way, so I couldn't keep up with it; and when I got to the depot the train was just starting."

" Pray, what took *you* to that neighborhood at that hour?" the silent man demanded so suddenly that the sound of his voice startled Walter.

If ever conscious guilt showed itself in a face, it now did in Walter's. He turned as red as a peony. Mr. Bright frowned, while the dark-skinned man smiled a knowing little smile.

"Why, nothing in particular, sir. I was only taking a little stroll about town, before going home," Walter replied, a word at a time.

"Yet your boarding place is at the other end of the city, is it not?" pursued Mr. Bright.

"Yes, sir, it is."

"Walter Seabury, up to this time I have always had a good opinion of you. This is no time for concealments. The house has been robbed of a large sum of money—so large that should it not be recovered within twenty-four hours we must fail. Do you hear —fail?" he repeated as if the word stuck in his throat and choked him.

"Robbed; fail!" Walter faltered out, hardly believing his own ears.

"Yes, robbed, and as I must believe by a scoundrel warmed at my own fireside. And you: why did you not report Ingersoll's flight before it was too late to stop him?"

Though shocked beyond measure by this

revelation, Walter made haste to reply: " Because, sir, I was not sure it was Ramon. It was just a look, and he was gone like a flash. Besides——"

" Besides what? "

" How could I know Ramon was running away? "

" Why, then, did you run after him? Are you in the habit of chasing every carriage you may chance upon in the street? " again interrupted the silent man.

Stung by the bantering tone of the stranger, Walter made no reply. Mr. Bright was his employer and had a perfect right to question him; but who was this man, and by what right did he mix himself up in the matter?

" Quite right of you, young man, to say nothing to criminate yourself; but perhaps you will condescend to tell us, unless it would be betraying confidence [again that cunning smile], if you knew that this Ingersoll was a gambler? "

The tell-tale blood again rushed to Walter's temples, but instantly left them as it dimly dawned upon him that he was suspected of knowing more than he was willing to tell.

" Gently, marshal, gently," interposed Mr. Bright. " He will tell all, if we give him time."

" One moment," rejoined the chief, with a meaning look at the merchant. " You hear, young man, this firm has been robbed of twenty thousand dollars—quite a haul. The thief has absconded. You tell a pretty straight story, I allow, but before you are many hours older you will have to explain why you, who have nothing to do with that department, should draw two thousand dollars at the bank yesterday; why, after getting banknotes you went back after gold," the marshal continued, warming up as he piled accusation on accusation; " why, again, you went from there to secure a berth in the *Georgia,* which sailed early this morning; and why you are seen, for seen you were, first watching Mr. Bright's house, and then arriv-

ing at the station just too late for the New
York express. Take my advice. Make a clean
breast of the whole affair. If you can clear
yourself, now is the time; if you can't, possibly you may be of some use in recovering the
money."

Walter felt his legs giving way under him.
At last it was all out. Now it was as clear
as day how Ingersoll had so craftily managed
everything as to make Walter appear in the
light of a confederate. Now he knew why
Ingersoll had wished to avoid being recognized. In a broken voice he told what he
knew of Ingersoll's wrong-doings, excusing
his own silence by the pledge he had given
and received.

When he had finished, the two men held
a whispered conference together. " Clear
case," observed the marshal; " one watched
your house while the other was making his
escape."

" I'll not believe it. Why, this young man
saved my daughter's life."

"Think as you like. At any rate, I mean to keep an eye on him." So saying, the marshal went on his way, humming a tune to himself with as much unconcern as if he had just got up from a game of checkers which he had won handily. At the street corner he hailed an officer, to whom he gave an order in an undertone, and then walked on, smiling and nodding right and left as he went.

Left alone with Mr. Bright, Walter stood nervously twisting his cap in both hands, like a culprit awaiting his sentence. It came at last. "Until this matter is cleared up," Mr. Bright said, "we cannot retain you in our employ. Get what is due you. You can go now." He then turned his back on Walter, and began busying himself over the papers on his desk.

Walter went out of the office without another word. He was simply stunned.

VII

THE FLIGHT

WALTER walked slowly down the wharf, feeling as if the world had suddenly come to an end. Nothing looked to him exactly as it looked one short hour ago. He did not even notice that a policeman was keeping a few rods behind him. As ¹e walked along with eyes fixed on the ground, a familiar voice hailed him with, "Why, what ails ye, lad? Seen a ghost or what?"

"Bill," said Walter, "would you believe it, that skunk of a Ramon has run off with a lot of the firm's money—to California, they say? And, oh, Bill! Bill! they suspect me, *me*, of having helped him do it. And I'm discharged. That's all." It was no use trying to keep up longer. Walter broke down completely at the sound of a friendly voice at last.

Bill silently led the way into the caboose. He first lighted his pipe, for, like the Indians, Bill seemed to believe that a good smoke tended to clear the intellect. He then, save for an occasional angry snort or grunt, heard Walter through without interruption. When the wretched story was all told Bill struck his open palm upon his knee, jerking out between whiffs: "My eye, here's a pretty kettle o' fish! Ruin, failure, crash, and smash. Ship ashore, and you all taken aback. Ssh!" suddenly checking himself, as a shadow darkened the one little pane of glass that served for a window. A policeman was looking in at them. Giving the two friends a careless nod, he walked slowly away.

It slowly dawned upon Walter that the man with the black rosette in his hat, whom he had seen at the office, had set a watch upon him. "Bill, you mustn't be seen talking to me," said Walter, rising to leave. "They'll think you are in the plot, too. Oh! oh! they dog me about everywhere."

The old fellow laughed scornfully. "That," he exclaimed, snapping his fingers, "for the hull b'ilin' on 'em. I've licked many a perleeceman in my time, and can do it again, old as I am. But we can be foxy, too, I guess. Listen. When I sees you comin', I'll go acrost the wharf to where that 'ar brig lays, over there. You foller me." Walter nodded. "I go up aloft. You follers. We has our little talk out in the maintop, free and easy like, and the perleeceman, he has his watch below."

When Walter reached his boarding house his landlady met him in the entry. She seemed quite flustered and embarrassed. "Oh, Mr. Seabury," she began, "I'm so glad you've come! Such a time! There has been an officer here tossing everything topsy-turvy in your room. He would do it, in spite of all I could say. I told him you were the best boarder of the lot; never out late nights, or coming home the worse for liquor, and always prompt pay. Do you think, he told me to shut up, and mind my own business. Oh, sir, what *is* the matter? That ever a nasty policeman should came ransacking in my house. Goodness alive! why, if it gets out, I'm a ruined woman. Please, sir, couldn't you find another boarding place?"

This was the last straw for poor Walter. Without a word he crept upstairs to his little bedroom, threw himself down on the bed, and cried as if his heart would break.

Walter was young. Conscious innocence helped him to throw off the fit of despondency; but in so far as feeling goes, he was ten years older when he came out of it. It was quite dark. Lighting a lamp, he hastily threw a few things into a bag, scribbled a short note to his aunt, inclosing the check received when he was discharged, settled with the landlady, who was in tears, always on tap; took his bag under his arm, and after satisfying himself that the coast was clear, struck out a round-about course, through crooked ways and blind alleys, to the wharf. For the life of him, he could not keep back a little bitter laugh when he called to mind that this was the second time in his short life that he had run away.

The wharf was deserted. There was no light in the caboose; but upon Walter's giving three cautious raps, the door was slid back, and as quickly closed after him. " Well," he said, wearily throwing himself down on a bench, " here I am again. I've been turned out of doors now. You are my only friend left. What would you do, if you were in my place? I can't bear it, and I won't," he broke out impulsively.

" I see," said Bill, meditatively shutting both eyes, to give emphasis to the assertion.

" Nobody will give me a place now, with a cloud like that hanging over me."

Bill nodded assent.

" I can't go back to the loft where I worked before, to be pointed at and jeered at by every duffer who may take it into his head to throw this scrape in my face. Would you? "

As Bill made no reply, but smoked on in

silence, Walter exclaimed, almost fiercely, " Confound it, man, say something! can't you? You drive me crazy with all the rest."

This time Bill shook the ashes from his pipe. " What would I do? Why, if it was me I'd track the rascal to the eends of the airth, and jump off arter him, but I'd have him. And arter I'd cotched him, I'd twist his neck just as quick as I would a pullet's," was Bill's quiet but determined reply.

Walter simply stared, though every nerve in his body thrilled at the bare idea. " Pshaw, you don't mean it. What put that silly notion into your head? Why, what could I do single-handed and alone, against such a consummate villain as that? Where's the money to come from, in the first place? "

Bill watched Walter's sudden change from hot to cold. " Jest you take down that 'ar coffee-pot over your head." Walter handed it to him, as requested. First giving it a vigorous shake, which made the contents rattle again with a metallic sound, Bill then raised the lid, showing to Walter's astonished eyes a mixture of copper, silver, and even a few gold, coins, half filling the battered utensil.

"Thar's a bank as never busts, my son," chuckled the old man, at the same time turning the coffee-pot this way and that, just for the pleasure of hearing it rattle. "What do you think of them 'ar coffee-grounds, heh? Single-handed, is it?" he continued, with a sniff of disdain. "I'll jest order my kerridge, and go 'long with ye, my boy."

It took some minutes for Walter to realize that Bill was in real, downright, sober earnest. But Bill was already shoving some odds and ends into a canvas bag to emphasize his decision. "Strike while the iron's hot" was his motto. Walter started to his feet with something of his old animation. "That settles it!" he exclaimed. "Since I've been turned out of doors, I feel as if I wanted to put millions of miles between me and every one I've ever known. Do you know, I think every one I meet is saying to himself, 'There's that Walter Seabury, suspected of robbing his employers'? Go away I must, but I've found out from the papers that no steamer sails before Saturday, and to-day is Wednesday, you know. Where shall I hide my face for a day or two? How do I know they won't arrest me, if they catch me trying to leave the city? Oh, Bill, I can never stand that disgrace, never!"

Having finished with his packing, Bill blew out the light, pushed back the slide, and gave a rapid look up and down the wharf. As he drew in his head, he said just as indifferently as if he had proposed taking a short walk about town, " 'Pears to me as if the correck thing for folks in our sitivation like was to cut and run."

"True enough for me. But how about you? They'll say that you were as deep in the mud as I am in the mire. Give it up, Bill. No, dear old friend, I mustn't drag you down with me. I can't."

" Bah! Talk won't hurt old Bill nohow. Bill's about squar' with the world. He owes just as much as he don't owe."

Walter was deeply touched. He saw plainly that it was no use trying to shake the old fellow's purpose, so forbore urging him further.

The old man waited a moment for Walter to speak, and finding that he did not, laid his big rough hand on the lad's shoulder and asked impressively, " Did you send off your chist to your aunt as I told ye to? "

" I did, an hour ago."

" An' did you kind o' explanify things to the old gal? "

" How could I tell her, Bill? Didn't she always say I would come to no good end? I wrote her that I was going away—a long way off—and for a long time. I couldn't say just how long. A year or two perhaps. My head was all topsy-turvy, anyhow."

" You didn't forgit she took keer on ye when ye war a kid? "

"I sent her the check I got from the store, right away."

"Then I don't see nothin' to——hender us from takin' that 'ar little cruise we was a-talkin' about."

It was pitch-dark when our two adventurers stepped out of the caboose. After securing the door with a stout padlock, Bill silently led the way to the stairs where he kept his wherry. Noiselessly the boat was rowed out of the dock, toward a light that glimmered in the rigging of an outward-bound brig that lay out in the stream waiting for the turning of the tide. Bill did not speak again until they were clear of the dock. "Yon brig's bound for York. I know the old man first-rate, 'cause I helped load her. He'll give us a berth if we take holt with the crew. Here we are." As he climbed the brig's side he set the wherry adrift with a vigorous shove of his foot.

A day or two after the events just described, Mr. Bright and the marshal met on the street, the former looking sober and down-cast, the latter smiling and elate. " What did I tell you? " cried the marshal, evidently well pleased with the tenor of the news he had to relate; " your *protégé* has gone off with an old wharf rat that I've had my eye on for some time."

" To tell you the whole truth, marshal, my mind is not quite easy about that boy," the merchant replied.

" Opportunity makes the thief," the officer observed carelessly.

" I'm afraid we've been too hasty."

" Perhaps so; but it's my opinion that when Ramon is found, the other won't be far off. I honor your feelings in this matter, sir, but my experience tells me that every rascal asserts his innocence until his guilt is proved. I've notified the police of San Francisco to be on the lookout for that precious clerk of yours. Good-day, sir."

When Mr. Bright returned to the store, on entering the office he saw an elderly woman, in a faded black bonnet and shawl, sitting bolt-upright on the edge of a chair facing the door, with two bony hands tightly clenched in her lap. There was fire in her eye.

"That is Mr. Bright, madam," one of the clerks hastened to say.

"What can I do for you, madam?" the merchant asked.

The woman fixed two keen gray eyes upon the speaker's face, as she spoke up, quite un-abashed by the quiet dignity of the merchant's manner of speaking.

"Well," she began breathlessly, "I'm real glad to see you if you have kept me wait-ing. Here I've sot, an' sot, a good half-hour. 'Pears to me you Boston folks don't get up none too airly fer yer he'lth. I was down here before your shop was open this mornin'. Better late than never, though."

The merchant bent his head politely. His visitor caught her breath and went on:

"I'm Miss Marthy Seabury. What's all this coil about my nevvy? He's wrote me

that he was goin' away.   Where's he gone?
What's he done?   That's what I'd like to
know, right up an' down."   She paused for
a reply, never taking her eyes off the merchant's troubled face for an instant.

"My good woman," Mr. Bright began in
a mollifying tone, when she broke in upon
him abruptly:

"No palaverin', mister.   No beatin' the
bush, if ye please.   Come to the p'int.   I left
my dirty dishes in the sink to home, an' must
go back in the afternoon keers."

"Then don't let me detain you," resumed
Mr. Bright gravely.   "There has been a
defalcation.   I'm sorry to say your nephew
is suspected of knowing more than he was willing to tell about it.   So we had to let him go.
Where he is now, is more than I can say."

"What's a defalcation?"

"A betrayal of trust, madam."

"Do you mean my boy took anything that
didn't belong to him?"

"Not quite that.   No, indeed.   At least, I

hope not. But, you see, Walter is badly mixed up with the precious rascal who did."

" Well, you'd better not. I'd like to see the man who'd say my boy was a thief, that's all. Why, I'd trust him long before the President of the United States! " The woman actually glared at every one in the office, as if in search of some one willing to take up her challenge.

" If you'll try to listen calmly, madam," interposed the merchant, " I'll try to tell you what we know." He then went on to relate the circumstances already known to us.

Aunt Martha gave an indignant sniff when the merchant had finished. " You call yourself smart, eh? Why, an old woman sees through it with one eye. Walter was just humbugged. So was you, warn't ye? An' goin' on right under your own nose ever so long, an' ye none the wiser for't. Well, I declare to goodness, if I was you I sh'ld feel real downright small potatoes! "

" I think, madam, perhaps we had better

bring this interview to a close.   It is a very painful subject, I do assure you."

" Very well, sir.   I sh'ld think you'd want to.   But mark my words.   You'll be sorry for this some day, as I am now that Walter ever laid eyes on you or—your darter." With this parting shot she bounced out of the office, shutting the door with a vicious bang behind her.

But Mr. Bright's worries that day were not to be so easily set at rest.   Upon reaching his home for a late dinner, looking pale and care-worn, it was Dora who met him in the hall-way, who put her arms round her father's neck, and who kissed him lovingly on both cheeks.

" Dear papa, I know all," she said with a little sob.

" Ah! " he ejaculated.   " Then you have heard——"

" Yes, papa; our next-door neighbor, Mrs. Pryor, has told me all about it.   Hateful old thing! "

The merchant made a gesture of resignation.

"She said you would have to discharge most of your clerks."

Mr. Bright made a gesture of assent.

"Then I want to do something. I can give music lessons. I'll work my fingers off to help. I know I shall be a perfect treasure. But why *did* you send Mr. Seabury away, papa?"

"Because he was unfaithful."

"I don't believe a word of it."

"Appearances are strongly against him."

"I don't care. I say it's a wicked shame. Why, what has he done?"

"What has he done? Why, he knew Ramon gambled, and wouldn't tell. He knew Ramon had gone, and never lisped a syllable."

"Yes, but that's what he didn't do."

"He was caught hanging around our house the night that Ramon ran away. There, child, don't bother me with any more questions.   Guilty or not, both have gone beyond reach."

Dora came near letting slip a little cry of surprise.   She knew that she was blushing furiously, but fortunately the hall was dark. A new light had flashed upon her.   And she thought she could guess why Walter had been lurking round their house on that, to him, most eventful night.   Although she had never exchanged a dozen words with him, he had won her gratitude and admiration fairly, and now she began to feel great pity and sorrow for the friendless clerk.

Hearing Dora crying softly, her father put his arm around her waist and said soothingly: " There, child, don't cry; we must try to bear up under misfortune.   But 'tis a thousand pities——"

" Well," anxiously.

" Well, if I had known all that in season, the worst might have been prevented."

" And now? "

" And now, child, your father is a ruined

man." So saying, the merchant hung up his hat and walked gloomily away.

Dora ran upstairs to her own room and locked herself in, leaving the despondent merchant to eat his dinner solitary and alone.

VIII

OUTWARD BOUND

" BEATS Boston, don't it? " said Bill to Walter, as the *Susan J.* was slowly working her way up the East River past the miles of wharves and warehouses with which the shores are lined.

" Maybe it's bigger, but I don't believe it's any better," was Walter's guarded reply.

As soon as the anchor was down, the two friends hailed a passing boatman, who quickly put them on shore at the Battery, whence they lost no time in making their way to the steamship company's office—Bill to see if he could get a chance to ship for the run to the Isthmus, Walter to get a berth in the steerage just as soon as Bill's case should be decided. So eager were they to have the matter settled that they would not stop even to look at the wonders of the town.

While waiting their turn among the crowd in the office, Bill's roving eye happened to fall on a big, square-shouldered, thick-set man who sat comfortably warming his hands over a coal fire in the fireplace, which he wholly monopolized, apparently absorbed in his own thoughts. It was now the month of December, and the air was chilly. Bill hailed him without ceremony. " Mawnin', mister. Fire feels kind o' good this cold mawnin', don't it ? "

The person thus addressed did not even turn his head.

Unabashed by this cool reception, Bill added in a lower tone, " Lookin' out for a chance to ship, heh, matey? "

At this question, so squarely put, a suppressed titter ran round the room. The silent man gave Bill a sidelong look, shrugged his shoulders, and absently asked, " What makes you think so ? "

"D'ye think I don't know a sailorman when I see one? Mighty stuck up, some folks is. Better get that Ingy-ink out o' yer hands ef yer 'shamed on it."

The silent man rose up, buttoned his shaggy buffalo-skin coat up to his chin, pulled his fur cap down over his bushy eyebrows, and strode out of the office without looking either to the right or the left.

"I say, you!" a clerk called out to Bill. "Do you know who you were talking to? That's the old man."

"I don't keer ef it's the old boy. Ef that chap ha'n't hauled on a tarred rope afore now, I'm a nigger; that's all."

"That was Commodore Vanderbilt, the owner of this line," the clerk retorted very pompously, quite as if he expected Bill to drop.

The general laugh now went against Bill. "Whew! was it, though? Then I s'pose my cake's all dough," he grumbled to himself, but was greatly relieved when the shipping clerk, after a few questions, told him to sign the articles. Walter was duly engaged, in his turn, as a cabin waiter. This being settled, the two friends sallied forth in high spirits to report on board the *Prometheus*, bound for San Juan del Norte.

Nowhere, probably, since the days of Noah was there ever seen such utter and seemingly helpless confusion as on one of those great floating arks engaged in the California trade by way of the Isthmus, in the early fifties, just before sailing. Bullocks were dismally lowing, sheep plaintively bleating, hogs squealing. Men were wildly running to and fro, shouting, pushing, and elbowing each other about, as if they had only a few minutes longer to live and must therefore make the most of their time. Women were quietly crying, or laughing hysterically, by turns, as the fit happened to take them. Of human beings, upwards of a thousand were thus occupied on board the *Prometheus;* while on the already crowded slip the shouting of belated hack drivers, who stormed and swore, the loud cries of peddlers and newsboys, who darted hither and thither among the surging throng, served to keep up an indescribable uproar. Add to this, that the sky was dark and lowering, the black river swimming with floating ice, crushing and grinding against the slip, as it moved out to sea with the ebb; and possibly some idea may be formed of what was taking place on that bleak December afternoon.

But all things must come to an end. All this confusion was hushed when the word was passed to cast off, the paddle wheels began slowly to turn, and the big ship, careening heavily to port under its human freight, who swarmed like bees upon her decks, forged slowly out into the stream, carrying with her, if the truth must be told, many a sorry and homesick one already.

Walter, however, drew a long breath of relief as the ship moved away from the shores. It was the first moment in which he had been able to shake off the fear of being followed. He therefore went about his duties cheerfully, if not very skillfully.

Oh, the unspeakable misery of that first night at sea! A stiff southeaster was blowing when the steamer thrust her black nose outside of Sandy Hook. And as the hours wore on, and the gale rose higher and higher, with every lurch the straining ship would moan and tremble like a human being in distress. Now and then a big sea would strike the ship fairly, sending crockery and glassware flying about the cabin with a crash, then as she settled down into the trough, for one breathless moment it would seem as if she would never come up again. Twenty times that night the affrighted passengers gave themselves up for lost. Most of them lay in their berths prostrated by fear or seasickness. A few even put on life preservers. Perhaps a score or more, too much terrified even to seek their berths, crouched with pallid faces on the cabin stairs, foolishly imagining that if the ship did go down they would thus have the

better chance of saving themselves.   Some
half-crazed women had even put on their bon-
nets, in order, as they sobbed out, to die
decently.

It was hardly light, if a blurred gray streak
in the east could be called light, when Walter
crept up the slippery companionway.   His
head felt like a balloon, his eyes like two
lumps of lead, his legs like mismatched legs.
The ship was working her engines just enough
to keep her head to the sea.   The deck was
all awash, and littered with the rubbish of a
row of temporary, or "standee," bunks
abandoned by their occupants, and broken
up by the force of the gale.   The paddle-
boxes were stove, and tons of water were
pouring in upon the decks with every revolu-
tion of the wheels.   By watching his chance,
when the ship steadied herself for another
plunge, Walter managed to work his way
out to the forepart of the vessel.   Here
he found Bill, with half a dozen more, all
wringing-wet, hastily swallowing, between

lurches of the ship, a cupful of hot coffee,
which the cook was passing out to them from
the galley. If ever men looked completely
worn out, then those men did.

Bill no sooner caught sight of Walter, than
he offered him his dipper. Walter put it
away from him with a grimace of disgust.

"Dirty night," said Bill, cooling his coffee
between swallows; "blowed fresh; nary
watch below sence we left the dock; no life
in her; steered like a wild bull broke loose in
Broadway. She's some easier now. Better
have some [again holding out his cup]; 't will
do you good. No? Well, here goes," tilting
his head back and draining the cup to the last
drop.

Just then the first officer came bustling
along in oilskins and sou'wester. "Here,
you!" he called out, "lay for'ard there, and
get the jib on her; come, bear a hand!" Walter went forward with the men. Hoisting
the sail was no easy matter, with the ship
plunging bows under every minute, but no

sooner did the gale fill it fairly, than away
it went with a report like a cannon, blown
clean out of the bolt-rope, as if it had been a
boy's kite held by a string.   While the men
were watching it disappear in the mist, crash
came a ton or more of salt water pouring over
the bow, throwing them violently against the
deck-house.   Shaking himself like a spaniel,
the mate darted off to give the steersman a
dressing-down for letting the ship " broach
to."

Two sailors had been lost overboard during the night.   On a hint dropped by Bill,
Walter was taken from the cabin, where there
was little to do, and put to work with the car-
penter's   gang,   repairing   damages.   The
change being much to his liking, Walter ap-
plied himself to his new duties with a zeal
that soon won for him the good will of his
mates.   And when it came to doing a job on
the rigging, though out of practice, Walter
was always the one called upon to do it.   The
captain, a quiet, gentlemanly man, who looked

more like a schoolmaster than a shipmaster, told the purser to put Walter in the ship's books.

Thoroughly tired out with his day's work, Walter was going below when the mate called out to him: " I say, youngster, you're not going down into that dog-hole again. There's a spare bunk in my stateroom. Get your traps and sail in. You can h'ist in as much sleep as you've storage room for."

By noon of the second day out, the *Prometheus* had run into the Gulf Stream. The gale had sensibly abated, though it still blew hard. When the captain came on deck, after taking a long look at the clouds, he said to the mate, " Mr. Gray, I think you may give her the jib and mainsail, to steady her a bit."

At break of day on the morning of the fourth day out, as Walter was leaning over the weather rail, his eye caught sight of a dark spot rising out of the water nearly abeam. The mate was taking a long look at it through his glass. In reply to Walter's inquiring look, the mate told him it was a low-lying reef called Mariguana, one of the easternmost of the Bahamas. It was not long before most of the passengers were crowding up to get sight of that little speck of dry land, the first they had laid eyes on since the voyage began. "Now, my lad, you can judge something of how Columbus felt when he made his first landfall hereabouts so long ago!" exclaimed the mate. "Good for sore eyes, ain't it? We never try to pass it except in the daytime," he added; "if we did, ten to one we'd fetch up all standing."

"San Domingo to-morrow!" cried the mate, rubbing his hands as he came out of the chart room on the fifth day. As the word passed through the ship it produced a magical effect among the passengers, whose chief desire was once more to set foot on dry land, and next to see it.

Sure enough, when the sun rose out of the ocean next morning there was the lovely tropic island looming up, darkly blue, before them. There, too, were the hazy mountain peaks of Cuba rising in the west. All day long the ship was sailing between these islands, on a sea as smooth as a millpond. Every day she was getting in better trim, and going faster; and the spirits of all on board rose accordingly at the prospect of an early ending of the voyage.

"This beats all!" was Walter's delighted comment to Bill, who was swabbing down the decks in his bare feet.

"'Tis kind o' pooty," Bill assented, wiping his sweaty face with his bare arm. "That un," nodding toward Cuba, "Uncle Sam ought to hev, by good rights; but this 'ere," turning on San Domingo a look of contempt, "'z nothin' but niggers, airthquakes, an' harricanes. Let 'em keep it, says Bill;" then continuing, after a short pause, "Porter Prince is up in the bight of yon deep bay. I seen the old king-pin himself onct. Coaltar ain't a patchin' to him; no, nor Day & Martin nuther. Hot? If you was ashore there, you'd think it was hot. Why, they cook eggs without fire right out in the sun."

A two-days' run across the Caribbean Sea brought the *Prometheus* on soundings, and a few hours more to her destined port. Every one was now making hurried preparations to leave the ship, bag and baggage; every eye beamed with delight at the prospect of escaping from the confinement of what had seemed more like a prison than anything else. While the *Prometheus* was heading toward her anchorage there was time allowed for a brief survey of the town and harbor of San Juan del Norte, or, as it was then commonly called, Greytown.

These were really nothing more than an open roadstead, bounded by a low, curving, and sandy shore, along which half a hundred poor cabins lay half hid among tall cocoanut palms. From the one two-story building in sight the British flag was flying. The harbor, however, presented a very animated and warlike appearance, in consequence of the warm dispute then in progress between England and the United States as to who should control the transit from ocean to ocean. Two American and two British warships lay within easy gunshot of each other, flying the flags of their respective nations, and no sooner were the colors of the starry banner caught sight of than a tremendous cheer burst from the thousand throats on board the *Prometheus*. Her anchor had hardly touched bottom when a boat from the *Saranac* came alongside, the officer in charge eagerly hailing the deck for the latest news from the States. As for the jackies, to judge from their looks they seemed literally spoiling for a fight.

Walter had no very clear idea upon the subject of this international dispute, still less of the importance it might assume in the future, but the evident anxiety shown on the faces around him led him to suppose that the matter was serious. He stood holding onto the lee rigging, watching the American tars in the boat alongside, and thinking what fine, manly fellows they looked, when two passengers near him began an animated discussion which set him to thinking.

"Sare," said one, with a strong French accent, "it was, *ma foi,* I shall recollect—*ah oui*—it was my countryman, one Samuel Champlain, who first gave ze idea of cutting —what you call him?—one sheep canal across ze Eesmus. I shall not be wrong today."

"Excuse me, monsieur," the other returned, "I think Cortez did that very thing long before him."

"Nevair mind, *mon ami.* I *gage* you 'ave ze *histoire* correct. Eet only prove zat great minds 'ave always sometime ze same ideas. *Mais,* your Oncle Sam, wiz hees sillee Monroe Doctreen, he eez like ze dog wiz his paw on ze bone: he not eat himself; he not let any oder dog: he just growl, growl, growl."

"But, monsieur, wouldn't Uncle Sam, as you call him, be a big fool to let any foreign nation get control of his road to California?"

The Frenchman only replied by a shrug.

Even before the *Prometheus* dropped anchor she was surrounded by a swarm of native boatmen, of all shades of color from sour cream to jet-black, some holding up bunches of bananas, some screaming out praises of their boats to such as were disposed to go ashore, others begging the passengers to throw a dime into the water, for which they instantly plunged, head first, regardless of the sharks which could be seen lazily swimming about the harbor, attracted by the offal thrown over from the ships.

"I don't know how 'tis," said Bill in Walter's ear, "but them sharks 'll never tech a nigger. But come, time to wake up! Anchor's down. All's snug aboard. Now keep your weather eye peeled for a long pull across the Isthmus."

"Good luck to ye," said the jolly mate, shaking Walter heartily by the hand as he was about leaving the ship. "I'm right glad to see you've been trying to improve your mind a bit, instead of moonin' about like a catfish in a mudhole, as most of 'em do on board here.   Use your eyes.   Keep your ears open and don't be afraid to ask questions. That's the way to travel, my hearty!"   And with a parting wave of the hand he strode forward.

IX

In the course of an hour or so three light-draught stern-wheel steamboats ("wheelbarrows," Bill derisively called them) came puffing up alongside. Into them the passengers were now unceremoniously bundled, like so many sheep, and in such numbers as hardly to allow room to move about, yet all in high glee at escaping from the confinement of the ship, at which many angrily shook their fists as the fasts were cast off. In another quarter of an hour the boats were steaming slowly up the San Juan River, thus commencing the second stage of the long journey.

For the first hour or two the travelers were fully occupied in looking about them with charmed eyes, as with mile after mile, and turn after turn, the wonders of a tropical

forest, all hung about with rare and beautiful
flowers, and all as still as death, passed before
them. But Bill, to whom the sight was not
new or strange, declared that for his part he
would rather have a sniff of good old Boston's
east wind than all the cloying perfumes of
that wilderness of woods and blossoms. It
was not long, however, before attention was
drawn to the living inhabitants of this fairy-
land.

First a strange object, something between
a huge lizard and a bloated bullfrog, was
spied clinging to a bush on the bank. No
sooner seen than crack! crack! went a dozen
pistol shots, and down dropped the dirty
green-and-yellow creature with a loud splash
into the river.

"There's a tidbit gone," observed Bill, in
Walter's ear.

"What! eat that thing?" demanded Walter with a disgusted look.

"Sartin. They eat um; eat anything.
And what you can't eat, 'll eat you. If you

don't b'leeve it, look at that 'ar reptyle on the bank yonder," said Bill, pointing out the object in question with the stem of his pipe.

Walter followed the direction of Bill's pipe.

Looking quite as much like a stranded log as anything else, a full-grown alligator lay stretched out along the muddy margin of the river at the water's edge. No sooner was he seen, than the ungainly monster became the target for a perfect storm of bullets, all of which glanced as harmlessly off his scaly back as hailstones from a slate roof. Disturbed by the noise and the shouts, the hideous animal slid slowly into the water and disappeared from sight, churning up the muddy bottom as he went.

Bill put on a quizzical look as he asked Walter if he knew why some barbarians worshiped the alligator. Walter was obliged to admit that he did not. " 'Cause the alligator can swaller the man, but the man can't swaller the alligator," chuckled Bill.

Now and then a native bongo would be overhauled, bound for San Carlos, Grenada, or Leon, with a cargo of European goods. They were uncouth-looking boats, rigged with mast and sail, and sometimes thirty to forty feet long. Many a hearty laugh greeted the grotesque motions of the jet-black rowers, who half rose from their seats every time they dipped their oars, and then sank back with a grunt to give their strokes more power. The *patrón,* or master, prefaced all his orders with a persuasive " Now, gentlemen, a little faster, if you please!"

" And so that's the way, is it, that all inland transportation has been carried on here for so many hundred years? " thought Walter. " Well, I never! "

Incidents such as these served, now and then, to cause a ripple of excitement, or until even alligators became quite too numerous to waste powder upon. As darkness was

coming on fast, there being no twilight to
speak of in this part of the world, a ship's
yawl was seen tied up under the bank for the
night. Its occupants were nowhere in sight,
but the dim light of a fire among the bushes
showed that they were not far off. "Run-
away sailors," Bill explained; "stole the boat,
an' 'fraid to show themselves. Poor devils!
they've a long pull afore 'em ef they get
away, an' a rope's-end behind 'em if they're
caught."

"Why, how far is it across?"

"It's more'n a hundred miles to the lake,
and another hundred or so beyond."

"Whew! you don't say. Well, I pity
them."

When darkness had shut down, the steamers also were tied up to trees on the bank,
scope enough being given to the line to let the
boats swing clear of the shores, on account
of the mosquitoes, with which the woods were
fairly alive. In this solitude the travelers
passed their first night, without other shelter

than the heavens above, and long before it
was over there was good reason to repent of
the abuse heaped upon the *Prometheus,* since
very few got a wink of sleep; while all were
more or less soaked by the rain that fell in
torrents, as it can rain only in the tropics,
during the night.   As cold, wet, and gloomy
as it dawned, the return of day was hailed
with delight by the shivering and disconsolate
travelers.   In truth, much of the gilding had
already been washed off, or worn off, of their
El Dorado.   And, as Bill bluntly put it, they
all looked "like a passel of drownded
rats."

Bill made this remark while he and Walter
were washing their hands and faces in the
roily river water, an easy matter, as they had
only to stoop over the side to do so, the boat's
deck being hardly a foot out of water.   Suddenly Walter caught Bill's arm and gave it a
warning squeeze.   Bill followed the direction in which Walter was looking, and gave
a low whistle.   A beautifully mottled black-

and-white snake had coiled itself around the line by which the boat was tied to the shore, and was quietly working its way, in corkscrew fashion, toward the now motionless craft. Seizing a boat-hook, Bill aimed a savage blow at the reptile, but the rope only being struck, the snake dropped unharmed into the river.

"Do they raise anything here besides alligators, snakes, lizards, and monkeys?" Walter asked the captain, who was looking on, while sipping his morning cup of black coffee.

Glancing up, the captain good-humoredly replied, "Oh, yes; they raise plantains, bananas, oranges, limes, lemons, chocolate-nuts, cocoanuts——"

"Pardon me," Walter interrupted; "those things are luxuries. I meant things of real value, sir."

"A very proper distinction," the captain replied, looking a little surprised. "Well, then, before you get across you will probably see hundreds of mahogany trees, logwood trees, fustic and Brazil-wood trees, to say nothing of other dye-woods, more or less valuable, growing all about you."

" Oh, yes, sir, I've seen all those woods you tell of coming out of vessels at home, but never growing. Somehow I never thought of them before as trees."

" Then there is cochineal, indigo, sugar, Indian corn, coffee, tobacco, cotton, hides, vanilla, some India rubber———"

Walter looked sheepish. " I see now how silly my question was. Please excuse my ignorance."

" That's all right," said the captain pleasantly. " Don't ever be afraid to ask about what you want to know. I suppose I've carried twenty thousand passengers across, and you are positively the first one to ask about anything except eating, sleeping, or when we are going to get there."

The two succeeding days were like the first, except that the river grew more and more shallow in proportion as it was ascended, and

the country more and more hilly and broken.
This furnished a new experience, as every now
and then the boats would ground on some
sand-bar, when all hands would have to tumble out into the water to lighten them over
the rift, or wade ashore to be picked up again
at some point higher up, after a fatiguing
scramble through the dense jungle. " Whew !
This is what I calls working your passage,"
was Bill's quiet comment, as he and Walter
stood together on the bank, breathing hard,
after making one of these forced excursions
for half a mile.

" Is here where they talk of building a
canal?" Walter asked in amazement, casting
an oblique glance into the pestilential swamps
around him. " Surely, they can't be in earnest."

" They'll need more grave-diggers than
mud-diggers, if they try it on," was Bill's em-
phatic reply. " White men can't stand the
climate nohow. And as for niggers—well,
all you can git out o' 'em's clear gain, like

lickin' a mule," he added, biting off a chew
of tobacco as he spoke.

On the afternoon of the third day the passengers were landed at the foot of the Castillio
Rapids, so named from an old Spanish fort
commanding the passage of the river at this
point, though many years gone to ruin and
decay. Walter and Bill climbed the steep
path leading up to it. The castle was of great
age, they were told, going back to the time of
the mighty Philip II of Spain perhaps, who
spent such vast sums in fortifying his American colonies against the dreaded buccaneers.
Walter could not help feeling awe-struck at
the thought that what he saw was already old
when the Pilgrims landed on Plymouth Rock.
Some one asked if this was not the place
where England's naval hero, Lord Nelson,
first distinguished himself, when the castle
was taken in 1780.

Leaving these crumbling ruins to the
snakes, lizards, and other reptiles which
glided away at their approach, the two went

back to the clump of rough shanties by the
river, and it was here that Walter made his
first acquaintance with that class of adventurers who, if not buccaneers in name, had
replaced them, to all intents, not only here
but on all routes leading to the land of gold.

There was a short portage around the
rapids. A much larger and more comfortable boat had just landed some hundreds of
returning Californians at the upper end of
this portage, and a rough-and-ready looking
lot they were, betraying by their talk and
actions that they had long been strangers to
the restraints of civilized life. Of course
every word they dropped was greedily de-
voured by the newcomers, by whom the Californians were looked upon as superior beings.

The two sets of passengers were soon exchanging newspapers or scraps of news, while
their baggage was being transferred around
the portage. Giving Walter a knowing
wink, Bill accosted one of the Californians
with the question, " I say, mister, is it a fact,

now, that you can pick up gold in the streets in San Francisco?"

"Stranger," this individual replied, "you may bet your bottom dollar you can. It's done every day in the week. You see a lump in the street, pick it up, and put it in your pocket until you come across a bigger one, then you heave the first one away, same's you do pickin' up pebbles on the beach, *sabe?*" Giving a nod to the half-dozen listeners, who were eagerly devouring every word, the fellow turned on his heel and walked off to join his companions.

The run across Lake Nicaragua was made in the night. When the passengers awoke the next morning the steamer was riding at anchor at a cable's length from the shore, on which a lively surf was breaking. Behind this was a motley collection of thatched hovels known as Virgin Bay. The passengers were put ashore in lighters, into which as many were huddled as there was standing-room for, were then hauled to the beach by means of a hawser run between boat and shore, and, with their hearts in their mouths while pitching and tossing among the breakers, at last scrambled upon the sands as best they might, thanking their lucky stars for their escape from drowning.*

Walter and Bill found themselves standing among groups of chattering half-breeds, half-nude children, dried-up old crones, and hairless, dejected-looking mules, whose shrill hee-haws struck into the general uproar with horribly discordant note. It was here bargains were made for the transportation of one's self or baggage across the intervening range of mountains to the Pacific. Secure in their monopoly of all the animals to be had for hire, the avaricious owners did not hesitate to demand as much for carrying a trunk sixteen miles as its whole contents were worth —more indeed than a mule would sell for.

* The picture is by no means overdrawn, as on a subsequent occasion, by the capsizing of a lighter in the surf, many passengers were drowned.

Walter was gazing on the novel scene with wide-open eyes. Already their little store of cash was running low.

"You talk to them, Bill; you say you know their lingo," Walter suggested, impatient at seeing so many of the party mounting their balky steeds and riding away.

Bill walked up to a sleepy-looking mule driver who stood nearby idly smoking his cigarette, and laying his hand upon the animal's flank, cleared his throat, and demanded carelessly, in broken Spanish, "Qui cary, hombre, por este mula?"

The animal slowly turned his head toward the speaker, and viciously let go both hind feet, narrowly missing Bill's shins.

"Wow! he's an infamous rhinoceros, este mula!" cried Bill, drawing back to a safe distance from the animal's heels.

"Si, señor," replied the unmoved muleteer. "Viente pesos, no mas," he added in response to Bill's first question.

"Twenty devils!" exclaimed Bill in

amazement, dropping into forcible English; "we don't want to buy him." Then resorting to gestures, to assist his limited vocabulary, he pointed to his own and Walter's bags, again demanding, "Quantos por este carga, vamos the ranch, over yonder?"

"Cinco pesos," articulated the impassive owner, between puffs.

"Robber," muttered Bill under his breath. Rather than submit to be so outrageously fleeced, Bill hit upon the following method of traveling quite independently. He had seen it done in China, he explained, and why not here? Getting a stout bamboo, the two friends slung their traps to the middle, lifted it to their shoulders, and in this economical fashion trudged off for the mountains, quite elated at having so cleverly outwitted the Greasers, as Bill contemptuously termed them. In fact, the old fellow was immensely tickled over the ready transformation of two live men into a quadruped. Walter should be fore legs and he hind legs. When tired, they could take turn and turn about. If the load galled one shoulder, it could be shifted over to the other, without halting. "Hooray!" he shouted, when they were clear of the village; "to-morrow we'll see the place where old Bill Boar watered his hoss in the Pacific."

"Balboa, Bill," Walter corrected. "No horse will drink salt water, silly. You know better. Besides, it wasn't a horse at all. 'Twas a mule."

Night overtook the travelers before reaching the foothills, but after munching a biscuit and swallowing a few mouthfuls of water they stretched themselves out upon the bare ground, and were soon traveling in the land of dreams.

The pair were bright and early on the road again, which was only a mule-track, deeply worn and gullied by the passing to and fro of many a caravan. It soon plunged into the thick woods, dropped down into slippery gorges, or scrambled up steep hillsides, where the pair would have to make a short halt to mop their brows and get their breath. Then they would listen to the screaming of countless parroquets, and watch the gambols of troops of chattering monkeys, among the branches overhead. Bill spoke up: " I don't believe men ever had no tails like them 'ar monkeys; some say they did: but I seen many a time I'd like to had one myself when layin' out on a topsail yard, in a dark night, with nothin' much to stan' on. A tail to kinder quirl around suthin', so's to let you use your hands and feet, is kind o' handy. Just look at that chap swingin' to that 'ar branch up there by his tail, like a trapeze performer, an' no rush o' blood to the brain nuther." Walter could hardly drag Bill away from the contemplation of this interesting problem.

For six mortal hours the travelers were shut up in the gloomy tropical forest; but just at the close of day it seemed as if they had suddenly stepped out of darkness into light, for far and wide before them lay the mighty Pacific Ocean, crimsoned by the setting sun.   Once seen, it was a sight never to be forgotten.

Walter and Bill soon pushed on down the mountain into the village of San Juan del Sur, of which the less said the better.   Thoroughly tired out by their day's tramp, the wayfarers succeeded in obtaining a night's lodging in an old tent, at the rate of four bits each. It consisted in the privilege of throwing themselves down upon the loose sand, already occupied by millions of fleas, chigoes, and other blood-letting bedfellows.   Glad enough were they at the return of day.   Bill's eyes were almost closed, and poor Walter's face looked as if he had just broken out with smallpox.

San Juan del Sur was crowded with people anxiously awaiting the arrival of the steamship that was to take them on up the coast. The only craft in the little haven was a rusty-looking brigantine, which had put in here for a supply of fresh water.   Her passengers declared that she worked like a basket in a gale of wind.   Learning that the captain was on shore, our two friends lost no time in hunting him up, when the following colloquy took place:

" Mawnin', cap," said Bill. " How much do you ax fur a cabin passage to 'Frisco?"

" A hundred dollars, cash in advance. But I can't take you; all full in the cabin."

" Well, s'pos'n I go in the hold; how much?"

" Eighty dollars; but I can't take you. Hold's full, too."

" Jerusalem! Why can't I go in the fore-peak? What's the price thar?"

" Eighty dollars; but I can't take you. Full fore and aft."

" 'Z that so? Well, say, cap, can't I go aloft somewhere? What 'll you charge then?"

" We charge eighty dollars to go any-where; but can't carry you aloft. Got to carry our provisions there."

Bill mused a minute. " Hard case, ain't it?" appealing first to Walter, then to the captain. " But as I want to go mighty **bad**, what 'll you tax to tow me? "

The captain turned away, with a horse-laugh and a shake of the head, to attend to his own affairs, leaving our two friends in no happy frame of mind at the prospect before them. With the utmost economy their little stock of money would last but little longer. The heat was oppressive and the place alive with vermin. Hours were spent on the harbor headland watching for the friendly smoke of the overdue steamer.

Several days now went by before the delayed steamer put in an appearance. It was none too soon, for with so many mouths to feed, the place began to be threatened with famine. It was by the merest chance that Walter secured a passage for himself in the steerage, and for Bill as a coal-passer, on this ship. Luckily for them, the captain's name happened to be the same as Walter's. He also hailed from New Bedford. He even admitted, though cautiously, that there might be some distant relationship. So Walter won the day, with the understanding that he was to spread his blanket on deck, for other accommodations there were none; while before the ship was two days at sea, men actually fought for what were considered choice spots to lie down upon at night.

The event of the voyage up the coast was a stay of several days at Acapulco, for making repairs in the engine room and for coaling ship. What a glorious harbor it is! land-locked and so sheltered by high mountains, that once within it is difficult to discover where a ship has found her way in, or how she is going to get out. Here, in bygone times, the great Manila galleons came with their rich cargoes, which were then transported across Mexico by pack-trains to be again reshipped to Old Spain. The arrival of a Yankee ship was now the only event that stirred the sleepy old place into life. At the sound of her cannon it rubbed its eyes, so to speak, and woke up. Bill even asserted that the people looked too "tarnation" lazy to draw their own breath.

Ample time was allowed here for a welcome run on shore; and the arrival of another steamer, homeward bound, made Acapulco for the time populous. Bill could not get shore leave, so Walter went alone. There were a custom-house without custom, a plaza, in which the inhabitants had hurriedly set up a tempting display of fruits, shells, lemonade, and home-made nicknacks to catch the passengers' loose change, besides a moldy-looking cathedral, whose cracked bells now and again set a whole colony of watchful buzzards lazily flapping about the house-tops. And under the very shadow of the cathedral walls a group of native Mexicanos were busily engaged in their favorite amusement of gambling with cards or in cock-fighting.

After sauntering about the town to his heart's content, Walter joined a knot of passengers who were making their way toward the dilapidated fort that commands the basin.

On their way they passed a squad of bare-
footed soldiers, guarding three or four vil-
lainous-looking prisoners, who were at work
on the road, and who shot evil glances at the
light-hearted Americanos. Walter thought
if this was a fair sample of the Mexican army,
there was no use in crowing over the victories
won by Scott and Taylor not many years before.

At the end of a hot and dusty walk in the
glare of a noonday sun, the visitors seated
themselves on the crumbling ramparts of the
old fort, and fell to swapping news, as the
saying is. One of the Californians was being teased by his companions to tell the story
of a man lost overboard on the trip down
the coast; and while the others stretched
themselves out in various attitudes to listen,
he, after lighting a cheroot, began the story:

"You know I can't tell a story worth a
cent, but I reckon I can give you the facts if
you want 'em. There was a queer sort of
chap aboard of us who was workin' his pas-

sage home to the States. We know'd him
by the name of Yankee Jim, 'cause he answered to the name of Jim, and said as how he
come from 'way down East where they pry
the sun up every morning with a crowbar.
He did his turn, but never spoke unless spoken
to. We all reckoned he was just a little mite
cracked in the upper story. Hows'ever, his
story came out at last."

X

ONE scorching afternoon in July, 185—, the Hangtown stage rumbled slowly over the plank road forming the principal street of Sacramento City, finally coming to a full stop in front of the El Dorado Hotel. This particular stage usually made connection with the day boat for " The Bay "; but on this occasion it came in an hour too late, consequently the boat was at that moment miles away, down the river. Upon learning this disagreeable piece of news, the belated passengers scattered, grumbling much at a detention which, each took good care to explain, could never have been worse-timed or more inconvenient than on this particular afternoon.

One traveler, however, stood a moment or two longer, apparently nonplused by the situ-

ation, until his eye caught the word " Bank "
in big golden letters staring at him from the
opposite side of the street.   He crossed over,
read it again from the curbstone, and then
shambled in at the open door.   He knew not
why, but once within, he felt a strange desire
to get out again as quickly as possible.   But
this secret admonition passed unheeded.

Before him was a counter extending across
the room, at the back of which rose a solid
wall of brick.   Within this was built the
bank vault, the half-open iron door disclosing
bags of coin piled upon the floor and shelves
from which the dull glitter of gold-dust
caught the visitor's eye directly.   The middle
of the counter was occupied by a pair of tall
scales, of beautiful workmanship, in which
dust was weighed, while on a table behind it
were trays containing gold and silver coins.
A young man, who was writing and smoking
at the same time, looked up as the stranger
walked in.   To look at the two men, one
would have said that it was the bank clerk

who might be expected to feel a presentiment of evil. Really, the other was half bandit in appearance.

Although he was alone and unnoticed, yet the stranger's manner was undeniably nervous and suspicious. Addressing the cashier, he said: " I say, mister, this yer boat's left; can't get to 'Frisco afore to-morrow " (inquiringly).

" That's so," the cashier assented.

" Well," continued the miner, " here's my fix: bound home for the States [dropping his voice]; got two thousand stowed away; don't know a live *hombre* in this yer burg, and might get knifed in some fandango. See? "

" That's so," repeated the unmoved official. Then, seeing that his customer had come to an end, he said, " I reckon you want to deposit your money with us? "

" That's the how of it, stranger. Lock it up tight whar I kin come fer it to-morrow."

" Down with the dust then," observed the cashier, taking the pen from behind his ear and preparing to write; but seeing his customer cast a wary glance to right and left, he beckoned him to a more retired part of the bank, where the miner very coolly proceeded to strip to his shirt, in each corner of which five fifty-dollar "slugs" were knotted. An equal sum in dust was then produced from a buckskin belt, all of which was received without a word of comment upon the ingenuity with which it had been concealed. A certificate of deposit was then made out, specifying that James Wildes had that day deposited with the Mutual Confidence and Trust Company, subject to his order, two thousand dollars. Glancing at the scrap of crisp paper as if hardly comprehending how that could be an equivalent for his precious coin and dust, lying on the counter before him, Jim heaved a deep sigh of relief, then crumpling the certificate tightly within his big brown fist, he exclaimed: "Thar, I kin eat and sleep now, I reckon. Blamed if I ever knew afore what a coward a rich man is!"

Our man, it seems, had been a sailor before the mast. When the anchor touched bottom, he with his shipmates started for the " diggings," where he had toiled with varying luck, but finding himself at last in possession of what would be considered a little fortune in his native town. He was now returning, filled with the hope of a happy meeting with the wife and children he had left behind.

But while Yankee Jim slept soundly, and blissfully dreamed of pouring golden eagles into Jane's lap, his destiny was being fulfilled. The great financial storm of 185— burst upon the State unheralded and unforeseen. Like a thief in the night the one fatal word flashed over the wires that shut the door of every bank, and made the boldest turn pale. Suspension was followed by universal panic and dismay. Yankee Jim was only an atom swallowed up in the general and overwhelming disaster of that dark day.

In the morning he went early to the bank, only to find it shut fast, and an excited and threatening crowd surging to and fro before the doors. Men with haggard faces were talking and gesticulating wildly. Women were crying and wringing their hands. A sudden faintness came over him. What did it all mean? Mustering courage to put the question to a bystander, he was told to look and read for himself. Two ominous words, " Bank Closed," told the whole story.

For a moment or two the poor fellow could not seem to take in the full meaning of the calamity that had befallen him. But as it dawned upon him that his little fortune was swept away, and with it the hopes that had opened to his delighted fancy, the blood rushed to his head, his brain reeled, and he fell backward in a fit.

The first word he spoke when he came to himself was " Home." Some kind souls paid his passage to 'Frisco, where the sight of blue water seemed to revive him a little. Wholly possessed by the one idea of getting home, he shipped on board the first steamer, which happened to be ours, going about his duty like a man who sees without understanding what is passing around him.

My own knowledge of the chief actor in this history began at four o'clock in the morning of the third day out. The *California's* engines suddenly stopped. There was a hurried trampling of feet, a sudden rattling of blocks on deck, succeeded by a dead silence— a silence that could be felt. I jumped out of my berth and ran on deck. How well I can recall that scene!

The night was an utterly dismal one—cold, damp, and foggy. A pale light struggled through the heavy mist, but it was too thick to see a cable's length from the ship, although we distinctly heard the rattle of oars at some distance, with now and then a quick shout that sent our hearts up into our mouths. We listened intently. No one spoke. No one needed to be told what those shouts meant.

How long it was I cannot tell, for minutes

seemed hours then; but at last we heard the
dip of oars, and presently the boat shot out of
the fog within a biscuit's toss of the ship.   I
remember that, as they came alongside, the
upturned faces of the men were white and
pinched.   One glance showed that the search
had been in vain.

The boat was swung up, the huge paddles
struck the black water like clods, the huge
hulk swung slowly round to her helm.   But
at the instant when we were turning away,
awed by the mystery of this death-scene, a
cry came out of the black darkness—a yell of
agony and despair—that nailed us to the deck.
May I never hear the like again! " Save
me! for God's sake, save me!" pierced
through that awful silence till a hundred voices
seemed repeating it.   The cry seemed so near
that every eye instinctively turned to the spot
whence it proceeded—so near that it held all
who heard it in breathless, in sickening sus-
pense.   Had the sea really given up its
dead?

Before one could count ten, the boat was again manned and clear of the ship. How well I recall the bent figure of the first officer as he stood in the stern-sheets, with the tiller-ropes in his hand, peering off into the fog! I can still see the men springing like tigers to their work again, and the cutter tossing on the seething brine astern like a chip. Then the fog shut them from our view. But nevermore was that voice heard on land or sea. No doubt it was the last agonized shriek of returning consciousness as the ocean closed over Yankee Jim's head.

At eight bells we assembled around the capstan at our captain's call, when the few poor effects of the lost man were laid out to view. His kit contained one or two soiled letters, a daguerreotype of two blooming children hand in hand, a piece of crumpled paper, and a few articles of clothing not worth a picayune. I took notice that while smoothing out the creases in this scrap of paper, the captain suddenly became deeply attentive, then thoughtful, then very red. Clearing his throat he began as follows:

" It's an old sea custom to sell by auction the kit of a shipmate who dies on blue water. You all know it's a custom of the land to read the will of a deceased person as soon as the funeral is over.   The man we lost this morning shipped by his fo'castle or sea name—a very common thing among sailors; but I've just found out his true one since I stood here; and what's more I've found out that the man had been in trouble.   An idea strikes me that he found it too heavy for him.   God only knows.   But it's more to the point that he has left a wife and two children dependent upon him for support.   Gentlemen and mates, take off your hats while I read you this letter."

The letter, which bore evidence of having been read and read again, ran as follows:

" Oh, James! and are you really coming home, and with such a lot of money too?

Oh, I can't believe it all! How happy we shall be once more! It makes me feel just like a young girl again, when you and I used to roam in the berry pastures, and never coveted anything in the wide world but to be together. You haven't forgot that, have you, James? or the old cedar on the cliff where you asked me for your own wife, and the sky over us and the sea at our feet, all so beautiful and we so happy? Do come quick. Surely God has helped me to wait all this long, weary time, but now it seems as if I couldn't bear it another day. And the little boy, James, just your image; it's all he can say, ' Papa, come home.' How can you have the heart to stay in that wicked place? "

When the reading was finished some of the women passengers were crying softly. The men stood grimly pulling their long mustaches. After a short pause the captain read aloud the fatal certificate of deposit, holding it up so that all might see.

"Now, ladies and gentlemen," he went on, "you've heard the story and can put this and that together. When we get to Panama I'm going to write a letter to the widow. It's for you to say what kind of a letter it shall be. Now, purser, you may put up the certificate of deposit."

"How much am I offered—how much?" said the purser, waving the worthless bit of paper to right and left.

Ten, twenty, forty, fifty dollars were bid before the words were fairly out of the purser's mouth. Then a woman's voice said seventy, another's one hundred, and the men, accepting the challenge, ran the bidding up fifty more, at which price the certificate was knocked down to a red-shirted miner who laid three fifty-dollar pieces on the capstan, saying as he did so: "'Tain't a patchin', boys. Sell her agin, cap—sell her agin."

So the purser, at a nod from the captain, put it up again, and the sale went on, each buyer in turn turning the the certificate over to the purser, until the noble emulation covered the capstan with gold.

"Stop a bit, purser," interrupted Captain M——, counting the money. "That will do," he continued. "The sale is over. Here are just two thousand dollars. The certificate of deposit is redeemed."

XI

IT was a fine, sunny afternoon when the *Pacific* turned her prow landward, and stood straight on for a break in the rugged coast line, like a hound with its nose to the ground. In an hour she was moving swiftly through the far-famed Golden Gate. A fort loomed up at the right, then a semaphore was seen working on a hilltop. In ten minutes more the last point was rounded, the last gun fired, and the city, sprung like magic from the bleak hillsides of its noble bay, welcomed the weary travelers with open arms. The long voyage was ended.

The wharf was already black with people when the steamer came in sight. When within hailing distance a perfect storm of greetings, questions, and answers was tossed from ship to shore. Our two friends scanned the unquiet throng in vain for the sight of one familiar face. No sooner did the gangplank touch the wharf than the crowd rushed pellmell on board. Women were being clasped in loving arms. Men were frantically hugging each other. While this was passing on board, Walter and Bill made their escape to the pier, hale and hearty, but as hungry as bears. Forty days had passed since their long journey began. What next?

Our two adventurers presently found themselves being hurried along with the crowd, without the most remote idea of where they were going. As soon as possible, however, Bill drew Walter to one side, to get their breath and to take their bearings, as he phrased it. " Well," said he, clapping Walter on the back, " here we be at last! "

Walter was staring every passer-by in the face. From the moment he had set foot on shore his one controlling thought and motive had come back to him with full force.

" Come, come, that's no way to set about
the job," observed the practical-minded Bill.
" One thing to a time. Let's get sumfin' t' eat
fust; then we can set about it with full stom-
achs. How much have you got? "

Walter drew from his pocket a solitary
quarter-eagle, which looked astonishingly
small as it lay there in the palm of his hand.
Bill pulled out a handful of small change,
amounting to half as much more.   " But coppers don't pass here, nor anything else under
a dime, I'm told," observed Walter.   " No
matter, they'll do for ballast," was Bill's reply, whose attention was immediately diverted
to a tempting list of eatables chalked upon the
door-post of a restaurant.   Beginning at the
top of the list, Bill began reading in an
undertone, meditatively stroking his chin the
while:

" ' Oxtail soup, one dollar.'   H'm, that
don't go down. ' Pigs' feet, one dollar each.'
Let 'em run. ' Fresh Californy eggs, one dollar each.'   Eggs is eggs out here. ' Corned

beef, one dollar per plate.' No salt horse for Bill. 'Roast lamb, one dollar.' Baa! do they think we want a whole one? 'Cabbage, squash, or beans, fifty cents.' Will you look at that! Move on, Walt, afore they tax us for smellin' the cookin'. My grief!" he added with a long face, as they walked on, "I'm so sharp set that if a fun'ral was passin' along, I b'leeve I could eat the co'pse and chase the mo'ners."

Fortunately, however, Bill was not driven to practice cannibalism, for just that moment a Chinaman came shuffling along, balancing a trayful of pies on his head. Bill was not slow in hailing the moon-eyed Celestial in pigtail, to which the old fellow could not resist giving a sly tweak, just for the fun of the thing: "Mawnin', John. Be you a Whig or Know-Nothin'?" at the same time helping himself to a juicy turn-over, and signing to Walter to do the same.

"Me cakes. Melican man allee my fliend. Talkee true. You shabee, two bitee?"

This last remark referred to the pie which Bill had just confiscated.

Sauntering on, jostling and being jostled by people of almost every nation on the face of the earth, they soon reached the plaza, or great square of the city. Not many steps were taken here, when the strains of delicious music floated out to them from the wide-open doors of a building at their right hand. Attracted by the sweet sounds of " Home, Sweet Home," our two wayfarers peered in, and to Walter's amazement at least, brought up as he had been at home, for the first time in his life he found himself gazing into the interior of a gambling-house, in full swing and in broad daylight, like any legitimate business, courting the custom of every passer-by.

" Walk in, gentlemen," said a suave-looking individual who was standing at the door. " Call for what you like. Everything's free here. Free lunch, free drinks, free cigars; walk in and try your luck."

" ' Walk into my parlor, sez the spider to

the fly,'" was Bill's ironical comment upon this polite invitation. "Walt," he continued, a moment later, "I'm 'feared we throw'd our money away on that Chinee. Here's grub for nothin'." If they had only known it, the person they were looking for was inside that gambling den at that very moment. After rambling about until they were tired, the two companions looked up a place in which to get a night's lodging—a luxury which cost them seventy-five cents apiece for the temporary use of a straw mattress, a consumptive pillow, and a greasy blanket. After making the most frugal breakfast possible, it was found that their joint cash would provide, at the farthest, for only one meal more. The case began to look desperate.

They were sitting on the sill of the wharf, silently ruminating on the situation, when the booming of a cannon announced the arrival of a steamer which had been signaled an hour earlier from Telegraph Hill. A swarm of people was already setting toward the plaza.

The movement of a crowd is always magnetic, so Walter and Bill followed on in the same direction.

When within two blocks of the plaza they saw a long zigzag line of men and boys strung out for that distance ahead of them, some standing, some leaning against a friendly awning, some squatted on the edge of the plank sidewalk, while newcomers were every moment lengthening out the already long queue.

"What a long tail our cat's got!" was Bill's pithy remark. "Be they takin' the census, or what?"

It was learned that all these people were impatiently waiting for the opening of the post-office, but how soon that event was likely to happen nobody could tell. So the men smoked, whistled, chaffed every late arrival, and waited.

On the instant Walter was struck with a bright idea. Charley had never written him one word, it is true; but as it was ten to one

Waiting for the opening of the mail. — *Page 160.*

everybody in the city would be at the post-
office during the day, this seemed as likely a
place as any to meet with him.   Shoving Bill
into a vacant place in the line, Walter started
toward the head of it, staring hard at every
one, and being stared at in return, as he
walked slowly along.   When nearing the
head, without seeing a familiar face, a man
well placed in the line sang out, " I say,
hombre, want a job? "

"What job? "

" Hold my place for me till I kin go git
a bite to eat."

" I would in a minute, only I can't stop.
I'm looking for some one," said Walter, starting on.

" You can't make five dollars no easier."

This startling proposition to a young fellow who did not know where his next meal
was coming from, hit Walter in his weak
spot.

" Talk fast.   Is it a whack? " the hungry
man demanded.   " I've been here two hours

a'ready; be back before you can say Jack Robinson."

This singular bargain being struck, Walter stepped into line, when his file-leader turned to him with the remark, "Fool you hadn't stuck out for ten. That man runs a bank."

" Does he?" Walter innocently inquired. "What kind of a bank?"

" Faro-bank."

A loud guffaw from the bystanders followed this reply.

As soon as the hungry man came back to claim his place, and had paid over his five dollars, Walter hurried off to where he had left Bill, who stopped him in his story with the whispered words, " I seed him."

"Him? Who? Not Charley?"

" No; t'other duffer."

Walter gave a low whistle. "Where? Here? Don't you see I'm all on fire?"

" Right here. Breshed by me as large as life, and twice as sassy. Oh, I know'd him in spite of his baird. Sez I to myself, ' Walk along, sonny, and smoke your shugarette. Our turn's comin' right along.' "

" Too bad, too bad you didn't follow him." Walter was starting off again, with a sort of blind purpose to find Ramon, collar him, and make him disgorge his ill-gotten gains on the spot, when Bill held him back. " Tut, tut, Walt," he expostulated, " if the lubber sees you before we're good and ready to nab him, won't he be off in a jiffy? Now we know he's here, ain't that something? So much for so much. Lay low and keep shady, is our best holt."

To such sound reasoning Walter was fain to give in. Besides, Bill now insisted upon staying in the line until he could sell out too. With a jerk of the thumb, he pointed to where one or two patient waiters were very comfortably seated on camp-stools, and in a husky undertone proposed finding out where camp-stools could be had. Taking the hint, Walter started off, instanter, in search of a dealer in camp-stools, with whom he quickly struck a bargain for as many as he could carry, by depositing his half-eagle as security. The stools went off like hot cakes, and at a good profit. Bill, too, having got his price, by patient waiting, the two lucky speculators walked away to the first full meal they had eaten since landing, the richer by twenty dollars from the morning's adventure. Bill called it finding money; " just like pickin' it up in the street."

XII

AN UNEXPECTED MEETING

IT was getting along toward the middle of the afternoon when the two newly fledged speculators turned their steps to the waterside, Bill to have his after-dinner smoke in peace and quiet, while scanning with critical eye the various craft afloat in that matchless bay. Something he saw there arrested his attention wonderfully, by the way he grasped Walter's arm and stretched out his long neck.

" Will you look! Ef that arn't the old *Argonaut* out there in the stream, I'm a nigger. The old tub! She's made her last v'y'ge by the looks—topmasts sent down, hole in her side big 'nuff to drive a yoke of oxen through. Ain't she a beauty?"

After taking a good look at the dismantled hulk, Walter agreed that it could be no other than the ship on which he and Charley met with their adventure just before she sailed. It did seem so like seeing an old friend that Walter was seized with an eager desire to go on board. Hailing a Whitehall boatman, they were quickly rowed off alongside, and in another minute found themselves once more standing on the *Argonaut's* deck. A well-grown, broad-shouldered, round-faced young fellow, in a guernsey jacket and skull-cap, met them at the gangway. There were three shouts blended in one:

" Walter! "

" Charley! "

" Well, I'm blessed! "

Then there followed such a shaking of hands all round, such a volley of questions without waiting for answers, and of answers without waiting for questions, that it was some minutes before quiet was restored. Charley then took up the word: " Why, Walt, old fel'," holding him off at arm's length, " I declare I should hardly have known you with that long hair and that brown face. Yes; this is the *Argonaut*. She's a storeship now; and I'm ship-keeper." He then went on to explain that most of the fleet of ships moored ahead and astern were similarly used for storing merchandise, some merchants even owning their own storeships. " You see, it's safer and cheaper than keeping the stuff on shore to help make a bonfire of some dark night."

" Don't you have no crew?" Bill asked.

" No; we can hire lightermen, same's you hire truckmen in Boston. All those stores you see built out over the water get in their goods through a trap-door in the floor, with fall and tackle."

It may well be imagined that these three reunited friends had a good long talk together that evening. Charley pulled a skillet out of a cupboard, on which he put some sliced bacon. Bill started a fire in the cabin stove, while Walter made the coffee. Presently the bacon began to sizzle and the coffee

to bubble. Then followed a famous clattering of knives and forks, as the joyous trio set
to, with appetites such as only California air
can create.

Walter   told   his   story   first.   Charley
looked as black as a thundercloud, as Ramon's
villainy was being exposed. Bill gave an
angry snort or grunt to punctuate the tale.
Walter finished by saying bitterly, "I suppose it's like looking for a needle in a
haystack."

"Not quite so bad as that," was Charley's
quick reply. "It's a pity if we three,"
throwing out his chest, "can't cook his goose
for him. Bill has seen him. Didn't you say
he gambled? Thought so. Oh, he won't
be lonesome; there's plenty more here of that
stripe. Gamblers, thieves, and sharks own
the town. They do. It ain't safe to be out
late nights alone, unless you've got a Colt or
a Derringer handy, for fear of the Hounds."

"The Hounds!" echoed Walter and Bill.

"Yes, the Hounds; that's what they call

the ruff-scuff here. There's a storm brewing," he added mysteriously, then suddenly changing the subject, he asked, "Where do you *hombres* ranch?"

"Under the blue kannerpy, I guess," said Bill in a heavy tragedian's voice.

"Not by a jugful! You'll both stop aboard here with me. I'm cap'n, chief cook, and bottle-washer. Bill's cut out for a lighterman, so he's as good as fixed. Something 'll turn up for Walt."

"What did you mean by ranching?" Walter asked.

"This is it. This is my ranch. You hire a room or a shanty, do your own cooking and washing, roll yourself up in your blanket at night and go it alone, as independent as a hog on ice. Oh, you'll soon get used to it, never fear, and like it too; bet your life. Women's as scarce as hens' teeth out here. You can't think it. Why, man alive, a nice, well-dressed lady is such a curiosity that I've seen all hands run out o' doors to get a sight of one passin' by. Come, Bill, bear a hand, and pull an armful of gunny-bags out of that bale for both your beds. Look out for that candle! That's a keg of blastin' powder you're settin' on, Walt! If I'd only known I was goin' to entertain company I'd 'a' swep' up a bit. Are you all ready? Then one, two, three, and out she goes." And with one vigorous puff out went the light.

When Bill turned out in the morning he found Charley already up and busying himself with the breakfast things. "What's this 'ere craft loaded with?" was his first question.

"Oh, a little of everything, assorted, you can think of, from gunny-bags to lumber."

Walter was sitting on a locker, with one boot on and the other in his hand, listening. At hearing the word lumber he pricked up his ears. "That reminds me," he broke in. "Bright & Company shipped a cargo out here; dead loss; they said it was rotting in the ship that brought it."

Charley stopped peeling a potato to ask her name.

"The *Southern Cross*."

"Bark?"

"Yes, a bark."

"Well, p'r'aps now that ain't queer," Charley continued. "That's her moored just astern of us. Never broke bulk; ship and cargo sold at auction to pay freight and charges. Went dirt cheap. My boss, he bought 'em in on a spec. And a mighty poor spec it's turned out. Why, everybody's got lumber to burn."

Charley seemed so glum over it that Walter was about to drop the subject, when Charley resumed it. "You see, boys," he began, "here's where the shoe pinches. I had scraped together a tidy little sum of my own, workin' on ship work at big wages, sometimes for this man, sometimes for that. I was thinkin' all the while of buying off those folks at home who fitted me out (Walt here knows who I mean), when along comes my boss and says to me, ' I say, young feller, you seem a busy sort of chap. I've had my eye on you some time. Now, I tell you what I'll do with you. No nonsense now. Got any dust?' 'A few hundreds,' says I. 'Well, then,' says he, ' I don't mind givin' you a lift. Here's this *Southern Cross* goin' to be sold for the freight. I'll buy it in on halves. You pay what you can down on the nail, the rest when we sell out at a profit. *Sabe?*' Like a fool I jumped at the chance."

"Well, what ails you?" growled the irrepressible Bill; "that 'ar ship can't git away, moored with five fathoms o' chain, can she? Pine boards don't eat nor drink nothin', do they?"

"Who said they did?" Charley tartly retorted. It was plain to see that with him the *Southern Cross* was a sore subject.

"Waal, 'tain't ushil to cry much over bein' a lumber king, is it?" persisted Bill, in his hectoring way. "Down East, whar I come from, they laugh and grow fat."

"You don't hear me through. Listen to this: My partner went off to Australia seven or eight months ago, to settle up some old business there, he said. I've not heard hide nor hair of him since. Every red cent I'd raked and scraped is tied up hard and fast in that blamed old lumber. Nobody wants it; and if they did, I couldn't give a clean bill o' sale. Now, you know, Walt, why I never sent you nothin'!"

Walter was struck with an odd idea. In a laughing sort of way, half in jest, half in earnest, he said, "You needn't worry any more about what you owe me, Charley; I don't; but if it will ease your mind any, I'll take as much out in lumber as will make us square, and give you a receipt in full in the bargain."

"You will?" Charley exclaimed, with great animation. "By George!" slapping his knee, "it's a bargain. Take my share for what I owe you and welcome."

"Pass the papers on't, boys. Put it in

black an' white; have everything fair and square," interjected the methodical Bill.

Charley brought out pen and ink, tore a blank leaf out of an account book, and prepared himself to write the bill of sale.

" Hold on! " cried Walter, who seemed to be in a reckless mood this morning. " Put in that I'm to have the refusal of the other half of the cargo for ninety days at cost price. In for a penny, in for a pound," he laughed, by way of reply to Charley's wondering look.

For a minute or two nothing was heard except the scratching of Charley's busy pen. Walter's face was a study. Bill seemed lost in wonder.

" There. Down it is," said Charley, signing the paper with a flourish. " 'Pears to me as if we was doin' a big business on a small capital this morning. And now it's done, what on earth did you do it for, Walt? "

" Oh, I've an idea," said Walter, assuming an air of impenetrable mystery.

" Have your own way," rejoined Charley,

whose mind seemed lightened of its heavy
load. " Here, Bill, you put these dirty dishes
in that bread pan, douse some hot water over
them—there! Now look in that middle
locker and you'll find a bunch of oakum to
wipe 'em with. Walter, you get a bucket of
water from the cask with the pump in it, on
deck, and fill up the b'iler."

Under Charley's active directions the
breakfast things were soon cleared away.
Walter then asked to be put on shore, giving
as a reason that he must find something to do
without delay. " Whereabouts do they dig
gold here? " he innocently asked.

At this question Charley laughed outright.
He then told Walter how the diggings were
reached from there, pointing out the steamboats plying to " up-country " points, and
then to distant Monte Diablo as the land-
mark of the route. " There ain't no actual
diggin's here in 'Frisco," he went on to say,
" but there's gold enough for them as is
willin' to work for it, and has sense enough

not to gamble or drink it all away. Mebbe
you won't get rich quite so fast, and then
again mebbe you will. *Quien sabe?*"

"Queer sitivation for a lumber king,"
grumbled Bill.

"I didn't come out here to get rich; you
know I didn't," said Walter excitedly, rising
and putting on his cap with an air of determination.

"Easy now," urged Charley, putting an
arm around Walter; "now don't you go running all over town in broad daylight after that
fellow. Better send out the town crier, and
done with it. That's not the way to go to
work. Do you s'pose a chap in his shoes
won't be keepin' a sharp lookout for himself?
Bet your life. Yes, sir-ee! Now, look here.
My idee is not to disturb the nest until we
ketch the bird. This is my plan. We three
'll put in our nights ranging about town,
lookin' into the gambling dens, saloons, and
hotels. If the skunk is hidin' that's the time
he'll come out of his hole, eh, Bill?"

"Sartin sure," was the decided reply.

"Well, then, Walt, hear to reason. Don't you see that if there's anything to be done, the night's our best holt to do it in?"

Walter was not more than half convinced. "Couldn't I have him arrested on the strength of the handbill Marshal Tukey got out, offering a reward, and describing Ramon to a hair? See, here it is," drawing it out of an inside pocket and holding it up to view. "I could swear to him, you know, and so could Bill."

"On a stack of Bibles," Bill assented.

"Let me see it," Charley demanded, rapidly running his eye over the precious document. "'Five hundred dollars reward!' Five hundred fiddlesticks! Why, he'd go five hundred better and be off in a jiffy, with just a nod and a wink from the officers to keep out of the way a while." Having expressed this opinion, Charley tossed the handbill on the table with a disdainful sniff.

Walter was dumb. He had actually thought for a whole month that the mere sight of this accusing piece of paper would make the guilty wretch fall on his knees and beg for mercy. And to be told now that it was only so much waste paper struck him speechless.

Charley again came to the rescue. " Come, come; don't stand there looking as if you'd lost every friend you had on earth, but brace up. If you'd wanted to have that robber arrested, you should have gone a different way to work—'cordin' to law."

" What's to be done, then? "

" My idee is like this. Californy law is no good, anyhow. It's on the side that has most dust. But here's three of us and only one of him. We can lay for him, get him into some quiet corner, and then frighten him into doing what we say. How's that? "

" Capital! Just the thing. I always said you had the best head of the three."

" All right, then," cried Charley in his old,

sprightly way; " I give you both a holiday, so you can see the sights. Walter, you take care that Bill don't get lost or stolen."

" Me take care o' him, you mean," Bill retorted.

Getting into the boat the two friends then pulled for the shore. Walter's first remark, as they slowly sauntered along, was: " What a wooden-looking town! Wooden houses, wooden sidewalks, plank streets. It looks as if everything had sprung up in a night."

And so it had. At this time the city was beginning to work its way out from the natural beach toward deeper water; for as deep water would not come to the city, the city had to go out to deep water. And as many of the coming streets were as yet only narrow footways, thrust out over the shallow waters of the bay, the entire ragged water-front seemed cautiously feeling its way toward its wished-for goal. Cheap one-story frame buildings were following these extensions of new and old streets, as fast as piles could be

driven for them, so that a famous clattering
of hammers was going on on every side from
morning to night.

The two friends soon had an exciting experience. Just ahead of them, a dray was
being driven down the wharf at a rapid rate,
making the loose planks rattle again. In
turning out to let another dray pass him, the
driver of the first went too near the edge of
the wharf, when the weight of horse and dray
suddenly tilted the loose planks in the air,
the driver gave a yell, and over into the dock
went horse, dray, and man with a tremendous
splash.

It was all done so quickly that Walter and
Bill stood for a moment without stirring.
Fortunately their boat was only a few rods
off, so both ran back for her in a hurry. A
few strokes brought them to where the frightened animal was still helplessly floundering
in the water, dragged down by the weight of
the dray. The man was first pulled into the
boat, dripping wet. Bill then cut the traces

with his sheath-knife, while the drayman held
the struggling animal by the bit. He was then
towed to the beach safe and sound. By this
time a crowd had collected. Seeing his res-
cuers pushing off, the drayman elbowed his
way out of the crowd, and shouted after them,
" I say, you, *hombres,* this ain't no place to
take a bath, is it? This ain't no place to be
bashful. Come up to my stand, Jackson and
Sansome, and ask for Jack Furbish."

" Is your name Furbish? " asked Bill, resting on his oars.

" Yes; why? "

" Oh, nothin', only we lost a man overboard
onct off Cape Horn. His name was Furbish."

" Well, 'twarn't me. I was lost overboard from Pacific Wharf. Jackson and
Sansome! Git up, Jim! " bringing his black-
snake smartly down on his horse's steaming
flanks.

XIII

IN WHICH A MAN BREAKS INTO HIS OWN
STORE, AND STEALS HIS OWN SAFE

WALTER'S idea, as far as he had thought it out, was to hold on to this lumber cargo until Mr. Bright could be notified just how the matter stood. Should the merchant then choose to take any steps toward recovering the cargo of the *Southern Cross,* Walter thought this act on his part might go far to remove the unjust suspicions directed against himself. For this reason he had secured, as we have seen, a refusal of the cargo long enough for a letter to go and return.

Walter now set about writing his letter, but he now found that what had seemed so simple at first was no easy matter. As he sat staring vacantly at the blank paper before him, tears came into his eyes; for again the trying scene in the merchant's counting-room rushed vividly upon his memory. An evil voice within him said, " Why should I trouble myself about those who have so ill-used me and robbed me of my good name?" Yet another, and gentler, voice answered, " Do unto others as you would that they should do unto you." Compressing his lips resolutely, he succeeded in writing a very formal letter, not at all like what he had intended. But the main thing was to make himself clearly understood. So he carefully studied every word before putting it down in black and white, as follows:

" MR. BRIGHT,

" *Sir:* This is to inform you of my being here. I could not bear to be suspected of dishonesty when I knew I was innocent of wrongdoing. So I left. This is to inform you that the *Southern Cross* is in charge of my friend Mr. Charles Wormwood. You may recollect him. He is a fine young man.

Between us, we've got hold of half the cargo, and I have the refusal of the other half for ninety days. The man who owns it has gone away. If you think it worth while, send directions to somebody here what to do about it. This is a great country, only I'm afraid it will burn up all the time.

> " Your true friend,
>
> " WALTER SEABURY."

While on his way uptown to post his letter, Walter heard a familiar voice call out, " Hi, *hombre!* lookin' for a job? " It was the drayman of yesterday's adventure, placidly kicking his heels on the tail of his dray.

Walter candidly admitted that he would like something to do. The drayman spoke up briskly: " Good enough. Not afraid of dirty hands? No? Good again. Got some *plata?* No? Cleaned out, eh? So was I. Say, there's a first-rate handcart stand, on the next corner above here, I've had my eye on for some time. More people

pass there in a day than any other in 'Frisco.
Talk biz.   That corner has been waiting for
you, or it would 'a' been snapped up long ago.
No job less than six bits.   You can make any-
where from five to ten dollars a day.   Come,
what do you say?   Do we hitch hosses or
not?"

Walter had a short struggle with his pride.
It did seem rather low, to be sure, to be pushing a handcart through the streets, like the
rag-men seen at home, but beggars should not
be choosers, he reflected.   So, putting his
pride in his pocket, the bargain was closed
without more words.

Certainly Walter's best friends would
hardly have known him when he made his
first appearance on the stand, bright and early
next morning, rigged out in a gray slouch hat,
red woolen shirt, and blue overalls tucked into
a pair of stout cowhide boots.   His face, too,
was beginning to show signs of quite a prom-
ising beard which Walter was often seen
caressing as if to make sure it was still there

overnight and which, indeed, so greatly altered his looks that he now felt little fear of being recognized by Ramon, should they happen to meet some day unexpectedly in the street.

Walter ranched with his employer in a loft. With a hammer, a saw, and some nails, he had soon knocked together a bunk out of some old packing boxes. In this he slept on a straw mattress also of his own make, with a pair of coarse blankets for bedclothes. Another packing box, a water pail, a tin wash-basin, towel, and soap comprised all necessary conveniences, with which the morning toilet was soon made. The bed required no making. Rather primitive housekeeping, to be sure; yet Walter soon learned, from actual observation, that a majority of the merchants, some of whom were reputed worth their hundreds of thousands, were no better lodged than himself.

On the whole, Walter rather liked his new occupation, as soon as his first awkwardness had worn off. Here, at any rate, he was his own master, and Walter had always chafed at being ordered about by boys no older than himself. Then, he liked the hearty, democratic way in which everybody greeted everybody. It made things move along much more cheerfully. Walter was attentive. Business was good. At the close of each day he handed over his earnings to his employer, who kept his own share, punctually returning Walter the rest. "You'll be buyin' out Sam Brannan one of these days, if you keep on as you're goin'," was Furbish's encouraging remark, as he figured up Walter's earnings at twenty-five dollars, at the end of the first week.

"Who's Sam Brannan?"

"Not know who Sam Brannan is?" asked the drayman, lifting his eyebrows in amazement. "He's reputed the richest man in 'Frisco. Owns a big block on Montgomery Street. Income's two thousand a day, they tell me."

Walter could only gape, open-mouthed, in astonishment. The bare idea of any one man possessing such unheard-of wealth was something that he had never dreamed of.

" Fact," repeated the drayman, observing Walter's look of incredulity.

The restaurant at which Walter took his meals, until circumstances suggested a change, was one of the institutions peculiar to the San Francisco of that day. An old dismantled hulk had been hauled up alongside the wharf, the spar-deck roofed over, and some loose boards, laid upon wooden trestles, made to serve the purpose of a table, while the ship's caboose performed its customary office of scullery and kitchen.

The restaurant keeper was evidently new to the business, for he was in the habit of urging his customers to have a second helping of everything, much to the annoyance of his wife, who did the cooking. This woman was one of the class locally known as Sydney

Ducks, from the fact that she had come from Australia under the sanction of a ticket-of-leave. She was fat, brawny, red-faced, and quick-tempered,—in fact, fiery,—and when out of sorts gave her tongue free license. The pair were continually quarreling at meal-times, regardless of the presence of the board-ers, some of whom took a malicious pleasure in egging on the one or the other when words failed them. But it happened more than once that, when words failed, man and wife began shying plates, or cups and saucers, at each other's head, which quickly cleared the table of boarders.

Walter stood this sort of thing stoically until, one noon, when he was just entering the dining room, a flat-iron came whizzing by him, narrowly missing his head. The lan-guage that accompanied it showed madam to be mistress of the choicest Billingsgate in pro-fusion. By the time a second flat-iron sailed through the door Walter was a block away, and still running. It was shrewdly surmised that man and wife had broken up housekeeping.

Meanwhile the search for Ramon was faithfully kept up, yet so far with no better success than if the ground had opened and swallowed him up. Nobody knew a person of the name of Ingersoll. No doubt he had assumed another less incriminating. A decoy letter dropped in the post-office remained there unclaimed until sent to the dead-letter office. "Fool if he hadn't changed his name," muttered Bill, as Walter and he stood at a street corner, looking blankly into each other's face.

They were taking their customary stroll uptown in the evening, when the big bell on the plaza suddenly clanged out an alarm of fire. There was no appearance of fire anywhere,—no shooting flames, no smoke, no red glare in the sky,—yet every one seemed flocking, as if by a common understanding, toward the Chinese quarter. Catching the prevailing excitement, the three friends pressed forward with the crowd, which at every step was visibly increasing. Upon reaching the point where the fire-engines were already hard at work, the crowd grew more and more dense, shouts and cries broke out here and there, lights were glancing hither and thither, and still no sign of fire could be detected. What could it all mean?

It meant that by a secret understanding among the firemen, winked at by the city authorities, the fire department was " cleaning out " the Chinese quarter, which had become an intolerable nuisance, dangerous to health on account of the filthy habits of the moon-eyed Celestials. The fire lads were only too willing to undertake the job, which promised to be such a fine lark, and at the first tap of the bells they had rushed their machines to the indicated spot, run their hose into the houses, and, regardless of the screams and howlings of the frightened inmates, who were wildly running to and fro in frantic efforts to escape, a veritable deluge of water was being poured upon them from a dozen streams, fairly washing the poor devils out of house and home, some by the doors, some by leaping out of the windows, and some by the roofs. Whenever one made his appearance, the shouts of the mob would direct the firemen where to point their powerful streams, which quickly sent the unresisting victim rolling in the dirt, from which he scrambled to his feet more dead than alive.

Meantime the Chinese quarter had been thoroughly drenched, inside and out, the terrified inhabitants scattered in every direction, their belongings utterly ruined either by water or by being thrown into the street pell-mell, and they themselves chased and hunted from pillar to post like so many rats drowned out of their holes by an inundation, until the last victim had fled beyond the reach of pursuit.

When the whole district had been thus depopulated the vast throng turned homeward in great good humor at having shown those

miserable barbarians how things were done in
civilized America.

Time slipped away in this manner, and
gradually the edge was being taken off from
the keenness of the search, though never completely lost sight of. Not a nook or corner
of the town had been left unvisited, and still
no Ramon. It was, even as Walter had first
described it, quite like looking for a needle in
a haystack.

One morning Walter was called to help
Furbish move some goods from a downtown
wharf to a certain warehouse uptown. The
owner was found standing among his belongings, which were piled and tossed about
helter-skelter, in a state of angry excitement,
which every now and then broke forth in muttered threats and snappy monosyllables, directed to a small crowd of bystanders who
had been attracted to the spot.

" There'll be some hanging done round
here before long," he muttered, scowling
darkly at two or three rough-looking men,

each armed with a brace of pistols, who stood with their backs against the door of the building from which the man's goods had been so hastily thrown out.

This building stood on one of the new streets spoken of in a former chapter as built out over the water, or on what was then known as a water-lot. It seems that the title to this lot was claimed by two parties. The late occupant had taken a lease from one claimant for a term of years, and had built a store upon the lot, wholly ignorant that another party claimed it. He had punctually paid his rent to his landlord every month, and was therefore dumfounded when, late one afternoon, the second claimant, armed with an order of a certain judge and accompanied by a sheriff's posse, walked into his store, and after demanding payment of all back rents, which was stoutly refused, promptly ejected the unfortunate tenant, neck and heels, from his place of business. His goods were then thrown out into the street after him, and the door locked against him, with an armed guard keeping possession. This was the state of things when Furbish and Walter arrived on the ground.

"It's a wicked shame," declared Walter indignantly.

"Makes business good for us," was Furbish's careless reply. Then lowering his voice, he added, "Talk low and keep shady. Mark my words. There'll be hanging done before long," thus unconsciously echoing the very words of the dispossessed tenant.

Walter took the hint. He stared, it is true, but went to work without further comment, though he could see that the sympathy of the crowd was clearly with the unfortunate tenant. When the last load had been carted away, the crowd slowly dispersed, leaving only the surly-looking guards on the spot.

"Is all out?" demanded Furbish of the merchant, nodding his head toward the empty building.

"All but my safe. I want that bad; but

you see these robbers won't let me in.   It was
too heavy for them to move, or they were too
lazy, and now they won't even let me take my
papers out of it.   Curse them! "

" Got the key? "

" Oh, yes!   That's all safe in my pocket.
But what's a man going to do with a key? "

" You want that safe bad? "

" I'd give a hundred dollars for it this
minute; yes, two hundred."

Furbish now held a whispered colloquy
with Walter.   " Do you think your friends
would take a hand? "

" Oh, I'll answer for them," was the ready
reply.

" Enough said."

A place of meeting was then fixed upon,
after which the three conspirators went
their several ways—Furbish to mature his
plan of action, the merchant to nurse his
new-found hopes, Walter to enlist his two
friends in the coming adventure.   Charley was in high spirits at the prospect.

Bill thought it a risky piece of business, but if his boys were going to take a hand in it he would have to go too. Charley put an end to further argument by declaring that it was a burning shame if a man couldn't go into his own store after his own property, law or no law. For his part, he was bound to see the thing through. Walter stipulated that there should be no violence used, and that he should not be asked to enter the building if it was found to be still in the hands of the sheriff's men.

Just at midnight a row-boat, with an empty lighter in tow, put off from the *Argonaut's* side, care being taken to keep in the deep shadows as much as possible. Not a word was exchanged as the tow was quietly brought to the place agreed upon, where it lay completely hidden from curious eyes, if any such had been abroad at that hour. As the lighter lightly grazed the wharf a dark figure stole cautiously out from the shadow cast by a neighboring warehouse, and dropped into the hands stretched out to receive it: still another followed, and the party, now complete, held a short council in whispers.

Furbish had reconnoitered the store, finding only one watchman on guard outside. Yet he was positive that there were two or more inside, as he had seen a light shining through a crevice in the window-shutters, which suddenly disappeared while he was watching it.

The evicted merchant then explained that this light must have come from the little office, at the right hand of the street door, where he usually slept. This information confirmed the belief that the men inside had turned in until their turn should come to relieve the guard outside. If this should prove true, the midnight intruders felt that they would have a more easy task than they had supposed. This, however, remained to be seen. After listening to a minute description of the store, inside and out, Furbish gave the signal to proceed.

Making the boat fast to the scow's stern, the latter was poled along in the shadows of the wharves until, under Bill's skillful guidance, she glided between the two piers which supported the building that the party was in search of.

All listened intently for any sound indicating that their approach had been detected. As all seemed safe, the scow was quickly made fast directly underneath the trap-door contrived for hoisting up merchandise into the store by means of a block and tackle secured to a stout rafter overhead—an operation at which Charley had often assisted. It was, therefore, through this same trap-door that the intruders now meant to effect an entrance. But a first attempt, very cautiously made, to raise it, proved it to be bolted on the inside. This contingency, however, had been provided against, for Charley now produced a large auger, on which he rubbed some tallow to deaden the sound, while the merchant held a dark lantern in such a way as to show

Charley where to use his tool to advantage.

Very cautiously, and with frequent pauses to listen, a large hole was bored next to the place where the bolt shot into the socket. Two or three minutes were occupied in this work. Charley then succeeded in drawing back the bolt with his fingers, a little at a time, when the trap was carefully lifted far enough to let the merchant squeeze his body through it, and so up into the store. As this was felt to be the critical moment, those who were left below listened breathlessly for any sound from above, as the trap was immediately lowered after the merchant passed through it.

It was, of course, pitch-dark in the store, but knowing the way as well in the dark as in the daytime, and being in his stocking-feet, the merchant stood only a moment to listen. Out of the darkness the sleeping watchmen could be heard snoring heavily away in the little corner office. Groping his way with cat-like tread, the merchant, with two or three quick turns of the wrist, screwed a gimlet into the woodwork of the office door, over the latch, thus securely fastening the sleepers in. Observing the same precautions, he then felt for the lock on the front door, and finding the key in the lock he turned it softly, putting the key in his pocket. Even should they awake, the watchmen inside the office could only get out by breaking down the door; while their comrade outside would be kept from coming to their assistance. The merchant had certainly shown himself not only to be a man of nerve, but no mean strategist.

The merchant having signaled that all was safe, all the rest of the party, except Walter, immediately joined him. The safe was speedily located, some loose gunny-bags were spread upon the floor to deaden the sound, two stout slings were quickly passed around the safe, the tackle hooked on, and in less than ten minutes the object of the adventure was safely lowered into the lighter. No time was lost in getting the scow clear of her dangerous berth, nor was it until they had put a long stretch of water behind them that the adventurers breathed freely.

The daring midnight burglary was duly chronicled in the evening papers as one of the boldest and most successful known to the criminal annals of San Francisco. Would it be believed, it was asked, that with three heavily armed guards on the watch inside and outside of the building, the burglars had actually succeeded in carrying off so bulky an article as an iron safe under the very noses of these alleged guardians? Connivance on their part was strongly hinted at. The police were on the track of the gang who did the job, and the public might rest assured that when caught they would be given short shrift. The burglars were supposed to have sunk the safe in the harbor after rifling it of its contents.

XIV

CHARLEY AND WALTER GO A-GUNNING

CHARLEY frequently came ashore in the evening, leaving Bill in charge of the ship. Walter ranched at Clark's Point, near the waterside, and only a few steps from the landing place. The neighborhood, to tell the truth, did not bear a very good reputation, it being a resort for sailors of all nations, whose nightly carousals in the low dramshops generally kept the place in an uproar till morning, and often ended in bloodshed.

Walter was busily engaged in sewing up a rip in his overalls, meantime humming to himself snatches of " The Old Folks at Home," when Charley came stamping into the room. Seating himself on an empty nail-keg, he proceeded to free his mind in the following manner:

" You've been working pretty steady now for—how long? "

" Three months last Monday," assisted Walter, consulting a chalk mark on the wall.

" Long 'nuff to entitle you to a bit of a vacation, I'm a-thinkin'. What say to takin' a little gunnin' trip up country? Bill knows the ropes now pretty well. A friend of mine 'll lend me the shootin' fixin's. Couldn't you get off for a few days, think? Come, get that Ramon chap out of your head for a bit. It's wearin' on you."

Walter jumped at the offer. Thus far he had never set foot out of the city, and Charley, an enthusiast in anything that he had set his mind upon, now portrayed the delights of a tramp among the foothills of the Coast Range in glowing colors. Walter easily found a substitute for the few days he expected to be away, while Charley had nobody's permission to ask. So the very next afternoon saw the two sportsmen crossing the ferry to Contra Costa, Charley carrying a rifle and Walter a shotgun, the necessary traps for camping out being divided equally between them.

" I only hope we may set eyes on a grizzly," Charley remarked, slapping the breech of his rifle affectionately, as they stepped on shore. " That's why I chose this feller," he added.

" Better let grizzlys alone. From all I hear they're pretty tough customers," was Walter's cautious comment.

" I don't care. Just you wait till I see one, that's all. I'm all fixed for him—lock, stock, and barrel."

They soon struck into the well-beaten road leading to the Coast Range, and after steadily tramping until dark entered a small settlement where travelers, coming and going over this route, usually put up for the night. A night's lodging was soon arranged for at the only public house that the place could afford, and after eating a hearty supper, and leaving word with the landlord to call them up as soon as it was light in the morning, the two amateur hunters were glad to tumble into bed.

The house was a two-story frame building, with the second-story windows in front opening upon a veranda, after the Southern style of public houses. The air being hot and close in their room, Walter threw up a window the first thing upon going into it. He saw that one might easily step out from the room onto the veranda, or in, for that matter. Then, there was no lock on the door, but as neither he nor Charley was afraid of being robbed, the want of a lock did not prevent their going to sleep as soon as they struck their beds. It is probable that they did not even turn over once during the night.

Walter was awakened by the sound of a gentle scratching, or tapping, at the door. Upon opening his eyes he perceived that it was beginning to be quite light. He listened until the sound was repeated, sat up in bed, and being satisfied that it must be some one calling them to get up, slipped out of bed, yawning and stretching himself, went to the door, half opened it, and, still only half awake, peered out.

What he saw made him start back in affright, and his hair to rise up on his head in an instant.

Standing erect on his hind feet, clumsily beating the air with his forepaws and lolling out a long red tongue, was an enormous, shaggy grizzly bear at least a foot taller than Walter himself.

One look was enough. Giving one yell, Walter made a dash for the open window, leaped out upon the veranda, vaulted over it, and grasping firm hold of the railing, let himself drop down into the street. Imagining that the bear was close behind, he incontinently took to his heels, not even turning to look back over his shoulder to see what had become of Charley.

Startled out of a sound sleep by Walter's cry of alarm, Charley threw off the bedclothes, rubbed his eyes, and, with their aid, saw the bear waddling with rolling gait into the room on all fours. He too made a dash for the window, adopting without hesitation the only route of escape open to him.

The bear quickly followed suit, sliding with ease down an upright, and, on touching the ground, immediately set off after the fugitives, upon whom the discovery that the bear was after them acted like a spur upon a mettled charger. They no longer ran, they flew.

Up to this hour the village had not shaken off its slumbers, but the frantic shouts of the fugitives, who saw that the faster they ran the faster ran the bear, quickly aroused other sleepers from their morning nap. Dogs began to bark and give chase to the bear. Windows began to be thrown up, and heads to appear at them. Still the race for life continued. Bruin was evidently gaining upon the fugitives, who could not much longer keep up the pace at which they were going. Feeling his breath failing him, Char-

The hunters hunted by a grizzly bear. — *Page 208.*

ley, who was a few rods behind Walter, had even almost made up his mind to stop short in his tracks, face about, and let the bear work its will upon him, so giving his bosom friend a chance to escape.

Fortunately, however, this heroic self-sacrifice was not to be made. At the last house a street door was seen very cautiously to open, while a head protruded from it. Ceremony here was quite out of the question. Walter instantly dashed into this welcome haven of refuge, with Charley, now quite spent, at his heels, overturning the man of the house in their mad rush for safety. It took but a moment to shut and bolt the door, and, as if that was not enough, Walter braced his back against it, panting and breathless. Only when this was done, did the two friends draw a free breath. Both were completely done up.

Excited by the chase, enraged at seeing his victims escaping, the bear snuffed the air, pawed at the door, swayed his huge bulk to and fro, and gave vent to his rage in loud and unearthly roarings that could be heard by every inhabitant of the village.

Meantime the man into whose premises the two young men had so unceremoniously entered, after taking a good look at the bear out of the window, almost bent double in the effort to control his laughter. "Why, boys," said he, between fits of choking, "that's Jem Stackpole's tame grizzly." He had recognized the animal now holding them besieged as one that had been taken when a cub, and brought up by the landlord of the public house from which the boys had made their sudden exit, as an object of curiosity to his guests. The iron collar which Bruin still wore confirmed this account. It was all plain enough now. Having contrived to free himself from his chain, the bear had easily gained access to the house by climbing up the before-mentioned veranda bear-fashion. He was considered quite harmless, the man explained, but on seeing the young men run away the bear had run after them, at first out of mere playfulness. So Walter and Charley had been running a race with a tame grizzly, through the public street of the village, in broad daylight, in their night clothes.

By this time something of a crowd had collected, all tongues going at once. The laugh of course went against the boys, though some were in favor of shooting the bear, and so putting an end to his wild pranks. His master, however, who now came forward with a pitchfork in one hand and an earthenware dish containing a stiff mixture of whisky and honey in the other, objected to having the bear killed, although the creature was now so ferocious that no one dared to go near him.

Setting the dish down upon the ground, and silently waving the crowd back, the man began calling the bear by his pet name of "Rusty" in a coaxing tone, and presently Bruin, having scented the seductive mixture, marched toward it and began lapping it up, occasionally emitting a fierce growl by way of notifying the bystanders to keep their distance.

By the time the dish was licked clean Bruin was dead-drunk and rolling helplessly in the dirt. His chain was then securely fastened on, and the brute ignominiously dragged off to the stable to sleep off his potations.

Walter and Charley were compelled to borrow a pair of trousers apiece before they could venture back to the public house, the observed of all observers. Needless to say, they made all haste to leave the inhospitable spot. Upon calling for their bill, the landlord declared there was nothing to pay, and, with a straight face, politely hoped they would recommend his house to their friends.

Walter insisted upon paying, but the landlord was firm. The fame of the tame-bear hunt would attract customers to his house, he said. Under the circumstances he could not think of making any charge whatever.

When they were well out of the village, Charley, who had maintained a dogged silence, suddenly turned to Walter and exclaimed, " I won't tell if you won't! "

" Don't be a ninny," was the curt reply.

" If I'd only had my rifle! " muttered Charley, who, all the same, could not forbear looking backward every few minutes as they trudged on.

The disconsolate pair made their way up among the foothills, but neither seemed to be in the right mood for keen sportsmen, or else game was not so plenty as they had expected to find it. After Charley had blown the nipple out of his rifle in firing at a coyote, and Walter had shot half a dozen rabbits, which, though wounded, succeeded in reaching their holes and crawling into them, the twain willingly turned their faces homeward. Footsore and weary, but with appetites sharpened by their long tramp, they were only too glad to set foot once again in the streets of the city. With a brief " So long, Charley," " So long, Walt," " Mum, you know," " Hope to die," they separated to go their respective ways.

XV

WHILE on his way to work on Saturday morning, full of his own thoughts, Walter could not help noticing the absence of the usual bustle and movement in the streets. If the shops had not been open, he would have thought it was Sunday, instead of the last day of the week. All business seemed to be at a standstill. Merchants stood outside their doors, glancing uneasily up and down the street and from time to time holding whispered talks with their neighbors. Every one wore a sober face; every one seemed expecting something to happen. But what was it? What could it be?

Yesterday Walter would have passed along the same streets hardly noticed. To-day he wondered why everybody stared at him so.

Furbish was about starting off on his dray
when Walter reached the stand. He, too,
hardly replied when Walter gave him the customary "Good-morning." What could it all
mean?

Suddenly the big bell on the plaza
thundered out three heavy strokes — one,
two, three, and no more — boom! boom!
boom!

To the last day of his life Walter never
forgot the sight that followed. At the first
stroke of that deep-toned bell the strange
quiet burst its bounds. Those already in the
streets started off on the run for the plaza.
Those who were indoors rushed out, buckling
on their weapons as they ran. Workmen
threw down their tools to join in the race.
Furbish jumped off his dray, shouting to Walter as he ran, "Come on! Don't you hear
it?" There was no noise except the trampling of feet. Nobody asked a question of his
neighbor. But every eye wore a look of grim
determination, as if some matter of life and

death dwelt in the imperious summons of that loud alarm-bell.

After gazing a moment in utter bewilderment, Walter started off on the run with the rest. He, too, had caught the infection. The distance was nothing. He found the plaza already black with people. Beyond him, above the heads of the crowd, he saw a glittering line of bayonets; nearer at hand men were pouring out of a building at the right, with muskets in their hands. Walter stood on tiptoe. Some one was speaking to the crowd from an open window fronting the plaza, but Walter was too far off to catch a single word. The vast throng was as still as death. Then as the speaker put some question to vote, one tremendous " aye " went up from a thousand throats. It was the voice of an outraged people pronouncing the doom of evil-doers.

By the gleam of satisfaction on the faces around him, Walter knew that something of unusual moment had just been decided upon.

Burning with curiosity he timidly asked his nearest neighbor what it all meant. First giving him a blank look the man addressed curtly replied, "Get a morning paper," then moved off with the crowd, which was already dispersing, leaving the plaza in quiet possession of a body of citizen soldiers, with sentinels posted, and the strong arm of a new power uplifted in its might. That power was the dreaded Vigilantes, organized, armed, and ready for the common protection.

Though terribly in earnest, it was by far the most orderly multitude Walter remembered ever having seen, and he had seen many. In the newspaper he read what everybody else already knew, that one of the most prominent citizens had been brutally murdered in cold blood by a well-known gambler, in a crowded street and at an early hour of the previous evening. The victim's only provocation consisted in having spoken out like a man against the monstrous evils under which the law-abiding citizens had so long and so silently been groaning. This murder was the last straw. The murderer had been promptly taken by members of the secret Committee of Vigilance; the trial had been swift; and the hangman's noose was being made ready for its victim. The account closed with a burning appeal to all law-abiding citizens, at every cost, to rid the city of the whole gang of gamblers, thieves, and out-laws infesting it like a plague. "When the sworn officers of the law are so notoriously in league with such miscreants, nothing is left for the people but to rise in their might. *Vox populi, vox Dei!* Down with the Hounds!"

Charley and Bill were quietly eating their noonday meal, when Walter burst into the *Argonaut's* cabin in a state of wild excitement. Without stopping to take breath, he rapidly related what he had seen and heard that morn-ing, while his listeners sat with wide-open eyes until the tale was finished.

For a few moments the three friends stared

at each other in silence. Ever prompt, Charley was the first to break it. Jumping to his feet, he struck the haft of his knife on the table with such force as to set the dishes rattling, then waving it in the air he cried out exultingly, " Now we've got him ! " As the others made no reply except to look askance, he went on to say, " Don't you see that, foxy as he is, Ramon will be smoked out of his hole ? Didn't I tell you there would be hanging before long ? Why, there won't be one of his kidney left in 'Frisco inside of a week."

" You're right," said Walter, " for as I came along I saw men putting up posters ordering all criminals out of the city, on pain of being put on board an outbound vessel and shipped off out of the country."

" Good enough for 'em, too. The heft of 'em is Sydney Ducks an' ticket-o'-leave men, anyhow," quoth Bill, with a shake of the head.

" Hark ! " commanded Walter, holding up

his hand for silence. Even as he spoke, the deep tones of a bell came booming across the water. At that moment the bodies of two condemned murderers were swinging from crossbeams from an upper window of the plaza.

"If we're ever going to catch that chap, we'd better set about it before it's too late. What's to hinder our working this Vigilante business a little on our own hook? Nothing. Who's going to ask any questions? Nobody. Do you catch my idee?" questioned Charley.

Without more words the three friends hastened on shore, Walter leading the way to his stand. They had agreed not to separate again, and were busy talking over their plans when a Chinaman came up to Walter and slipped a paper in his hand. Walter ran his eye over it, then crushed it in his hand. Turning to the Chinaman he simply said, "All right, John; I'll be there."

"Allee light," repeated the Chinaman, making off into the crowd.

Walter drew the heads of his two friends close to his own. Then he whispered: "What do you think? This is an order to take some things from a certain house on Dupont Street to a warehouse on Long Wharf, at ten o'clock to-night. (Night work's double pay.) I can't be mistaken. The order is in *his* handwriting; I could swear to it."

"I consait we orter follow the Chinee," Bill suggested tentatively.

"No," objected Charley. "Prob'ly he'd lead us a wild-goose chase all over town. If Walter's right, we're hot on the scent now. Don't muddy the water, I say. The eel's a slippery cuss, and might wiggle away. Bill, let's you and I go take a look at that warehouse. Walt, don't you let on that you suspicion a thing. Why, you're all of a tremble, man! Straighten out your face. Anybody could read it like a book. Pull yourself together. Look at me! By jings, I feel like a fighting-cock just now!"

"What a bantam!" muttered Bill, following in Charley's springing footsteps.

At ten o'clock Walter was at the door of the house on Dupont Street with his cart. His knock was answered by the same Chinaman who had brought him the note in the morning. Several parcels were brought out and placed in the cart, but still no sign of the owner. The Chinaman then explained, in his pigeon English, that this person would meet Walter at the warehouse on the wharf, for which place Walter immediately started, revolving in his own mind whether this was not some trick of Ramon's contriving to throw him, Walter, off the scent.

Nobody appeared to answer Walter's knock at the warehouse door. Evidently it was deserted, but a low whistle gave notice that Charley and Bill were close at hand. Indeed, so well had they concealed themselves that Walter had passed on without seeing them.

"Have you got the rope all right, Bill?"

Walter nervously whispered, as the three crouched in the friendly shadow of a narrow passageway, while waiting for their victim to show himself.

"Sartin," that worthy calmly replied, "and all I wish is that what's-his-name was on one eend, and I on t'other."

"I don't half like this way of doing things; looks too much like kidnapping," Walter whispered, half to himself.

"Come, Walt, you're not going to show the white feather now, after all this trouble, I hope," Charley impatiently said. "Ssh! here he comes. It's now or never."

Sure enough, the sound of approaching footsteps was now plainly heard. As Ramon came nearer, walking fast, Bill, stepping out of the shadows, slowly lurched along ahead, cleverly imitating the zigzag walk of a tipsy sailor—no unusual sight at that time of night. When Ramon had passed a few rods beyond their hiding place, Charley quietly slipped out behind him, taking care to tread as softly as one of Cooper's Indians on the warpath. This plan had been carefully devised, for fear that Ramon might give an alarm if they attempted, all at once, to rush out upon him unawares. They now held their intended victim, as it were, between two fires.

At that hour the street was so lonely and deserted that there was little fear of interruption, so Charley did not hurry. When Bill had reached the place agreed upon, where the street narrowed to a lane in which not more than two persons could walk abreast, he began to slacken his pace, so as to let Ramon come up with him. As nothing could be seen, at a few rods off, in that uncertain light, the signal agreed upon was to be given by Bill's striking a match, when Walter and Charley were to come up as rapidly as possible.

As Ramon tried to push on by Bill, that worthy placed himself squarely in the way, pulled out his pipe, and gruffly demanded a light. He acted his part so well as completely to disarm Ramon's suspicions, had he had any.

At being thus suddenly brought to a stand, Ramon attempted to shoulder Bill out of his path, but on finding himself stoutly opposed, he instinctively drew back a step.

" Refuse a gen'leman a light, does yer? Want a whole street to yourself, does yer? " sputtered Bill, obstinately holding his ground. Ramon made a threatening movement. " Shove! I dare ye, ye lubber," continued the irate sailor, purposely raising his voice as his companion came in sight. " I'm a match for you any day in the week," he grumbled, striking a light as if to enforce the challenge.

By the light of the match Bill instantly recognized Ramon. At the same moment Ramon saw that the speaker was a total stranger. Charley barred the way behind him. Ramon's first thought had been that he was being waylaid by footpads and, instinctively his hand went to his pistol; but as no demand was made for his valuables, he quickly concluded it to be a chance encounter with a couple of tipsy sailors. A street row was the very thing he most dreaded. He was in a fever to be off. Then the thought struck him that perhaps he might turn these fellows to his own advantage. So he altered his tone at once. "Oh, it's all right, lads," he said apologetically, "but one must be careful in these times, you know; and you certainly did give me a start. Never mind. If you've got a boat handy, I'll make this the best night's work you ever did in the whole course of your lives."

Charley, who had edged up closer, now nudged Bill to hold his tongue. Speaking thickly, Charley said: "If you wants a boat we've got the one we was just goin' off in aboard ship. She lays right here, just ahead of us. If you come down han'some, we're the lads you want. 'Nuff said."

Ramon was completely deceived. "All right, then. I've got some traps yonder.

They're waiting for me, I see. We'll get them, and you can set me aboard the *Flamingo*. Hurry up! I've no time to lose."

Walter was nonplused when he saw the trio approaching in so friendly a manner. He was about to say something, when Charley trod sharply on his foot to enforce silence. All four then went down to the boat with Ramon's luggage. After handing Walter a gold piece, Ramon stepped lightly into the boat, Bill shipped the oars, and Charley took the tiller. Walter first cast off the painter, gave the boat a vigorous shove, and then leaped on board himself. He could not make out what had happened to change their plans, but this was no time for explanations.

Seeing the supposed cartman get into the boat, it then first flashed upon Ramon that he had been tricked. Half rising from his seat, he made a movement as if to leap overboard, but a big, bony hand dragged him backward. Maddened to desperation, Ramon then reached for his revolver, but before he could draw it, Walter threw his arms around him, and held him fast in spite of his struggles. Meantime Bill was taking two or three turns round Ramon's body with a stout rope, brought along for that very purpose, and in a twinkling that worthy found himself bound and helpless.

No word was spoken until the boat touched the *Argonaut's* side. Thoroughly cowed, shivering with cold and fright, Ramon's terror was heightened by the thought that he was being carried off to sea. As the black hull of the *Argonaut* loomed up before him the dreadful truth seemed to break upon him clearly. Yes, there was no doubt of it: he was being shanghaied, as the forcible kidnaping of sailors was called.

Charley went up the side first. In a minute he reappeared with a lighted lantern. A dull numbness had seized Ramon. He did not even attempt to cry out when Charley called to the others, in a guarded undertone, to " pass him along." Four stout arms then lifted, or rather boosted, Ramon on board the vessel, as limp and helpless as a dead man. "I knew it," he groaned, with chattering teeth; "shanghaied, by all that's horrible!"

XVI

CHARLEY at once led the way into the cabin. When all four had passed in he shut the door, turned the key in the lock, and set down the lantern on the table, when, by its dim light, Ramon saw, for the first time, the faces of his abductors. Stealing a quick glance around him he met Walter's set face and stern eye. The faces of the others gave him as little encouragement. Greatly relieved to find his worst fears unfounded, his courage began to rise again. He met Walter's look with one of defiance, and inwardly resolved to brazen it out. His life, he knew, was safe enough. To show that he was not afraid, he assumed a careless tone, as if he looked upon the whole thing as a joke.

"You've got me, boys. But now you've got me, what do you want with me?" he demanded, twisting a cigarette in his trembling fingers.

"First," said Walter, a trifle unsteadily, for the sight of his enemy was almost too much for him, "first we want you to sign this paper," taking it out of his pocket. "It is—you can read it—a full confession of your robbery of Bright & Company." In spite of his effrontery, Ramon could not help wincing a little. Walter went on without mercy, "And of your clever little scheme to throw suspicion on me as your accomplice." Ramon merely gave a contemptuous little shrug. "And lastly, of what you've done with all the property you — you stole." Ramon scowled and gnawed his mustache.

Now that he knew the worst, Ramon began to bluster. "Oh, you shall smart for this when I get on shore—yes, all of you," he declared hotly. "You've got the wrong pig by the ear this time; yes, you have. As for you," this to Bill, " you hoary-headed old villain, I'll have you skinned alive and hung up by the heels for a scarecrow."

Bill could hold in no longer. " Who said anything about your goin' ashore, I'd like to know? " he asked, in his bantering way. " You never 'd be missed, nohow. Here yer be, and here you stop till we've done with you. So none of your black looks nor cheap talk. They won't pass here."

" Stop me if you dare! It's abduction, kidnaping, felony! " cried Ramon, glancing fiercely from one face to the other. " I despise you and your threats. Where are your proofs? Where is your authority? "

" Ugly words those, big words. You want proofs, eh? What do you say to this? " Walter asked, in his turn, unfolding a handbill before Ramon's eyes with one hand, while with the other he held the lantern up so that the accusing words, in staring print, might be the more easily read:

STOP THIEF ! ! !
$500 REWARD !

The above reward will be paid for the apprehension of one Ramon Ingersoll, an absconding embezzler.

This was followed by a detailed description of his personal appearance.

" Now will you sign? " Walter again demanded of the branded thief and fugitive from justice.

Ramon smiled a sickly smile. " Oh! it's the reward you're after, is it? Hope you may get it, that's all."

At this fresh insult two red spots flamed up on Walter's cheeks. Ramon's dark eyes sparkled at having so cleverly seen through the motives of his captors.

" Is that your last word? "

" Before I'll sign that paper I'll rot right here! "

" You had better sleep on it," replied Walter, turning away.

"What! before s'archin' him for the steal-in's?" Bill asked, with well-feigned surprise, at the same time critically looking Ramon over from head to foot.

Ramon's hand went to his neckcloth, as if already he felt the hangman's noose choking him, the observant Bill meanwhile watching him as a cat does a mouse. "Come, my lad, turn out your pockets," he commanded, in a most business-like way.

Pale with anger, Ramon first pulled out a leather pocket-book, which he threw upon the table, with something that sounded very much like a muttered curse, after which he folded his arms defiantly across his chest. "Now you've got it, much good may it do you," he sneered.

The pocket-book contained only a few papers of little value to anybody.

"What has become of all the money you took?" Walter demanded.

"Gone," was the curt reply.

"What! gone! You can't have spent it

all so soon. Think again. There must be a trifle left."

Ramon shrugged his shoulders by way of reply.

"Feel for his belt, Bill," Charley struck in. Charley had been growing impatient for some time over so much waste of words. Bill hastened to take the hint.

"Hands off! I tell you, I'll not be searched," shouted Ramon, carrying his hands to the threatened spot like a flash. In spite of his struggles, however, the belt, which every one wore in that day, was secured, and in it ten new fifty-dollar gold pieces were found, and turned out upon the table. Again Ramon's hand went to his neckcloth, nervously, tremblingly. In a twinkling Bill had twitched that article off and tossed it to Walter. "Good's a belt, hain't it?" asked Bill in answer to Walter's look. "I seed him grabbin' at it twicet. S'arch it! s'arch it!"

Rolled up in a little wad, in the folds of the neckerchief, they found two certificates of

Ramon made to give up his stealings. — *Page 236.*

deposit of a thousand dollars each, and in another similar roll several notes of hand for quite large sums, made payable to Bright & Company, but with forged indorsements to a third party, who, it is needless to say, was no other than Ramon himself, who had thus added forgery to his catalogue of crime. Fortunately, his hurried departure had prevented the negotiating of these notes, which now furnished the most damning evidence of his misdeeds.

"Now, then," said Walter, sweeping the money and papers together in a heap, "we've drawn his teeth, let him bite if he can."

At this cutting taunt, Ramon summoned to his aid the remains of his fast-waning assurance. "Oho! my fine gentlemen, suppose I'm all you say I am, if you take my money you're as deep in the mud as I am in the mire; eh, my gallant highwaymen?" he hissed out.

"Enough of this. We shall take good care of you to-night; but to-morrow we mean to hand you over to the Vigilantes. You can then plead your own cause, Master Embezzler." So saying, Walter pointed to a stateroom opposite, to signify that the last word had been said.

Ramon's face instantly turned of a sickly pallor. As Bill afterwards said, " Walter's threat took all the starch out of him." In a broken voice he now pleaded for mercy. " I give it up. I'll confess. I'll sign all you say —anything—if you'll promise not to give me up to those bloodhounds," he almost whimpered. Truly, his craven spirit had at last got the mastery.

Walter pretended to hesitate, but in truth he was only turning over in his own mind how best to dispose of Ramon. Hitherto the wish for revenge had been strong within him, had really gone hand-in-hand with that to see wrong made right. But Ramon was now only an object of pity, of contempt. The confession was again placed before him with the addition of a clause stating that the money surrendered was the same he had taken from his employers. He himself added the words, "This is my free act and deed," after which he signed his full name as if in a hurry to have it over with. The two friends then witnessed it.

Walter put this precious document in his pocket with a feeling of real triumph. At last his good name would be vindicated before all the world. Once again he could look any man in the face without a blush. It seemed almost too good to be true, yet there sat Ramon cowering in a corner, while he, Walter, held the damning proofs of the robbery in his possession. No, it was not a dream. Right was might, after all.

Instead of asking to be set at liberty, Ramon now begged to be kept hid from the dreaded Vigilantes. "Give me just money enough to get away with, set me on shore after dark, and I'll take my chances," he pleaded. Only too glad to be well rid of him, the three friends willingly agreed to this proposal. After darkness had set in, Bill pulled Ramon to a distant spot above the town, among the sand dunes. Handing the discomfited wretch his own pocket-book, with the contents untouched, Bill gave him this parting shot: "Take it, and go to Guinea! If this is the last on ye, well an' good, but it's my 'pinion there's more rascality stowed away in that cowardly carkiss o' yourn." Without replying, Ramon stole away in the darkness, and was soon lost to sight.

XVII

A SHARP RISE IN LUMBER

" Isn't that the Sacramento boat? " asked Charley, looking off in the direction of a rapidly approaching bank of lights. " How plainly we can hear the drumming of her big paddles. Listen! "

" If it is, she's all of two hours ahead of time," was Walter's reply.

" Yes, it's the old *Senator's* day. She's a traveler all the time, and to-night she has the tide with her. Do you know, they say she's made more money for her owners than she could carry on one trip? "

" Sho! You don't mean it."

" True as you stand there."

They stood watching the *Senator* work her way into her dock, when Charley suddenly asked, "What are you so glum about to-night, Walt?"

"I was thinking what I would do if I had a boatload of money."

"Hope you may get it, that's all. Hark! Ah, here's Bill back again."

By the way that Bill was rowing, he seemed in a great hurry. Greatly to the surprise of the two friends, he was closely followed up the side by a stranger, to whom Bill lent a helping hand as this person stumbled awkwardly to the deck. At first both Walter and Charley thought it must be Ramon returning.

"Hello! what's up now?" both exclaimed in one breath.

"What's up? Lumber's up. Got any?" answered a quick, sharp voice not at all like Ramon's.

As nobody spoke Bill made a hurried explanation. "Sacramento's all burnt up, lock, stock, and barrel. Boat's goin' right back to-night. I seen her comin' lickety-split, fit to bust her b'iler; so I kinder waited round for the news. I heered this man askin' who had lumber, so I jest mittened onto him, and here he is."

"Whar's this yer lumber—afloat or on shore?" the newcomer impatiently demanded.

"Afloat," Charley replied.

"Good enough! How's it stowed: so's it can be got at?"

"It's a whole cargo. Never been broken out."

"Good again! What sort is it? Can I see it?"

"Come into the cabin and I'll get out the manifest. You can't see anything till daylight."

"Burn the manifest!" returned the stranger, still more impatiently. "Daylight's wuth dollars now. Show me the man can tell what that thar lumber is, or isn't."

"I can," Walter put in, "'cause I saw it loaded."

"Then you're the very man I want. Talk

fast. I'm bound to go back on that thar boat."

Thus urged, Walter began the inventory on his fingers. "There's six two-story dwelling houses, all framed, ready to go up."

"Whoop-ee! how big?"

"About 24x36, high-studded, pitched roof, luthern windows. The rest is building stuff —all of it—sills, joists, rough and planed boards, matched boards——"

"Any shingles?" the impatient man broke in.

"Yes, a big lot; and clapboards too."

"Talk enough. Whar's the owner?"

"You're talking to him now," said Charley quickly.

"Well, then, I reck'n we'd better have a little light on the subject, hadn't we?" the stranger suggested.

Upon this hint Charley led the way to the cabin, where the parties took a good look at each other. The stranger glanced over the manifest, laid a big, brawny hand upon it,

then, turning to Walter, but without betraying surprise at his youthful appearance, said
pointedly, "Name your price, cash down,
stranger, for the lot. I'm here for a dicker."

Walter began a rapid mental calculation.
"Those houses are worth all of twenty-five
hundred apiece," he declared, glancing at
Charley.

"More," Charley assented positively.

"Wuth more for firewood," added Bill.

"Houses and all; all or none. How much
for the hull blamed cargo?" the stranger
again demanded, getting up to expectorate
in a corner.

"Lumber is lumber," observed Charley,
wrinkling his forehead in deep thought.

"Do I ask you to give it away? Name
your figure," the would-be purchaser insisted.
"Come up to the scratch. I've no time to
waste here palavering. What do you take
me for?" he added angrily.

Walter again had recourse to his mental
arithmetic. "Six times two fifty, fifteen;

lump the rest at ten; freight money five, storage five more, insurance five. Forty thousand dollars!" he exclaimed desperately at a venture, feeling the cold sweat oozing out all over him.

"It's mine. I'll take it," said the stranger, coolly suiting the action to the word by dragging out of his coat pockets first one chuggy bag of gold dust and then another, which he placed before Walter on the table. "Here's something to bind the bargain." Then, seeing Bill critically examining a pinch of the dull yellow grains in the palm of his hand, he added: "Oh! never fear! That's the real stuff. You get the rest when that lumber's delivered alongside Sacramento levee at my expense. Talk fast. Is it a whack?"

"Hold on, stranger," cried the acute Charlay, pushing back the gold. "We don't agree to no such thing, mister. We deliver it right here from the ship."

The stranger smote the table with his clenched fist. "Can't waste no time loading and unloading," he declared; "that's half the battle. I must have this cargo ahead of everybody, up river. You say it's all loaded. That's why I pay high for it. I don't care shucks how you get it there; so fix it somehow; for it's make or break with me this time. *Sabe?*"

"Why not tow her up and back, if he pays for it?" Bill suggested.

The buyer caught as eagerly at the idea as a drowning man does at a straw. "Sartin. Tow her up!" he exclaimed. "I hire the boat and pay all expenses. How many hands of you? Three. All right. You get ten dollars apiece a day till the ship's unloaded."

The man's eagerness to buy his way through all obstacles rather confused Walter, who now turned inquiringly toward Bill.

"She draws nigh onto twenty feet this blessed minute," Bill said in a doubtful undertone.

"Why, the river is booming!" cried the stranger, looking from one to the other, with eager, restless eyes, as this unforeseen difficulty presented itself to his mind.

Again Bill came to the rescue. " I'll tell ye, mates, what we can do. Lash an empty lighter on each side of her; that 'll lift her some; then if she takes the ground, we might break out cargo into the lighters, till she floats agin."

The lumber speculator listened like one who hears some one speaking in a strange tongue. He, however, caught at Bill's idea. " Yes, that's the how, shoah," he joyfully assented. " I'll hire a towboat to-night, if one's to be had in 'Frisco for money. I don't know shucks 'bout these yer ships, but when it comes to steamboats I reck'n I kin tell a snag from a catfish."

" I think we may risk it, then," observed Charley, who, as ship-keeper, felt all his responsibility for her safety.

Walter then drew up the contract in proper form, after which it was duly signed, sealed, and witnessed.

"Now, then," resumed the stranger, "you boys get everything good and ready for a quick start. Thar's your dust. You play fa'r with me, an' I'll play fa'r with you. Shake."

He then put off with Bill for the shore.

"Dirt cheap," said Charley, eying Walter sidewise.

"Thrown away," groaned Walter peevishly, by way of reply.

And to think that only the day before the lumber would not have paid for the unloading!

XVIII

By dint of hard work the *Southern Cross* was got ready to cast off her moorings by the time the tug came puffing up alongside, early in the morning. They were soon under weigh, but the ship's bottom was so foul that she towed like a log.

Bill steered, while Charley and Walter went forward to pass the word from the tug or tend the hawser, as might be necessary. It being smooth water here, in an hour or so the tow passed out into San Pablo Bay, where it met not only a stiff head wind, but a nasty little choppy sea. That made towing slow work, but by noon they were abreast of Benicia and entering the Straits of Carquinez, with old Monte Diablo peering down upon them on the starboard hand.

Beyond this point the tow steamed across still another bay, for some fifteen miles more, without mishap. They had now left the coast mountains far behind, and were heading straight for what seemed an endless waste of tall reeds, through which both the Sacramento and San Joaquin wind their way out to the sea.

So far plenty of water and plenty of sea room had been found. The worst was yet to come. The young navigators, however, pushed boldly on between the low mud-banks without delay, feeling much encouraged by their success thus far, and wishing to make the most of the short two hours of daylight remaining, after which the captain of the tug declared it would be unsafe to proceed.

After seeing the ship tied up to the bank for the night, the tug pushed on in search of a wood-yard some miles farther on. It was quite ten o'clock the next morning before the boys saw her come puffing back around the next bend of the river above. She had run so far after wood, that the captain said he would not risk putting back before daylight again.

All went smoothly until the middle of the afternoon, when, to their great annoyance, the ship suddenly brought up on a mud-bank, where she stuck hard and fast. A hawser was quickly carried out astern, at which the tug pulled and hauled for some time to no purpose. The *Southern Cross* would not budge an inch.

It being evident that the ship would not come off by that means, hatches were taken off, the boys threw off their coats, and, spurred on by Bill's report that he believed the river was falling, all hands went to work breaking out cargo into the lighters, as if their very lives depended upon their haste. It was now that Bill's foresight came in for the warmest commendations, as without the lighters the voyage must have ended then and there.

They worked on like beavers all the rest of that afternoon, the tug giving an occasional pull at the hawser, without starting the ship from her snug berth. They, therefore, made themselves some coffee, and were talking the situation over in no very happy frame of mind, when a large, high-pressure steamboat was seen heading down the river, half of which she seemed pushing in front of her, and dragging the other half behind. " Stand by to haul away! " shouted Bill, with quick presence of mind, to the men on the tug, running aft to take another turn in the hawser. As the steamer passed by, churning the muddy water into big waves, the tug put on all steam, the hawser straightened out as tense as iron, the big ship gave a lazy lurch as a wave struck her, and to the unspeakable delight of all hands they found themselves once more afloat and in deep water.

Although the ship was aground several times after this, they were so lucky in getting her off, that by noon of the third day the *Southern Cross* lay snugly moored, stem and stern, to a couple of live oaks at the Sacramento levee. The first person to jump on board was the purchaser himself, followed by a gang of laborers, who had been waiting only for the ship's arrival to set to work at unloading her cargo. Meantime the boys set about making all snug aboard, and then after seeing the balance of the purchase money weighed out, on a common counter-scale in the cabin, they took turns in mounting guard over what had been so fairly earned. In plain truth, all three were fairly dazed by the possession of so much wealth.

This duty of standing watch and watch kept the friends from leaving the ship even for a single moment, if indeed they had felt the least desire to do so. In fact all that there was left of the late bustling city was spread out stark and grim before their wondering eyes from the deck of the ship, and a dismal sight it was. Acres of ground, so lately covered with buildings so full of busy life, were now nothing but a blackened waste of smoldering rubbish. Here and there some

Arrival of the *Southern Cross* at Sacramento.—*Page 254.*

solitary tree, scorched and leafless, lifted up its skeleton branches as if in silent horror at the surrounding desolation. Men, singly, or in little groups, were moving about in the gray-white smoke like so many uneasy specters. Others were carefully poking among the rubbish for whatever of value might have escaped the flames. But more strange than all, even while the ruins were ablaze about them, it was to see a gang of workmen busy laying down the foundations for a new building. There was to be no sitting down in sackcloth and ashes here. That was California spirit.

All this time the lumber dealer was by great odds the busiest man there. He was fairly up to his ears in business, selling lumber, in small parcels or great, from the head of a barrel, to a perfect mob of buyers, who pushed and jostled each other in their eagerness to be first served. All were clamoring as loudly for notice as so many Congressmen on a field-day to the Speaker of the House. To this horde of hungry applicants the lumberman kept on repeating, " First come, first served. Down with your dust." The man was making a fortune hand over fist.

Scarcely had our boys the time to look about them, when they were beset with offers to lease or even to buy the ship outright. One wanted her for a store, another for a hotel, another for a restaurant, a saloon, and so on. Men even shook pouches of gold-dust in their faces, as an incentive to close the bargain on the spot. As such a transaction had never entered their heads, the three friends held a hurried consultation over it. Charley firmly held to the opinion that he had no right to dispose of the ship without the owner's consent, and that was something which could not be obtained at this time. Walter was noncommittal. Bill was nothing if not practical. Bill was no fool.

" Ef she goes back, what does she do? " he asked, squinting first at one and then at the other. " Why, she lays there to

her anchors rottin', doin' nobody no good,"
he added.

" She won't eat or drink anything if she
does," Charley said rather ambiguously.

" Seems as though we ought to put her
back where we found her," Walter suggested,
in a doubtful sort of way.

" Settle it to suit yourselves," was Bill's
ready rejoinder. " But how does the case
stand? Here's a lot of crazy *hombres* e'en
a'most ready to fight for her. 'Twould cost
a fortin to get her ready for sea. Her bottom's foul as a cow-yard; some of her copper's torn off; upper works rotten; she needs
calkin', paintin', new riggin', new——"

" There, hold on! " cried Charley, laughing heartily at Bill's truly formidable catalogue of wants; " I give in. I vote to lease
the old barky by the month—that is, if Walt
here thinks as I do."

" In for a penny, in for a pound," Walter
assented decisively.

So the bargain was concluded before the

cargo was half out of the ship, so eager was the lessee to get possession. Walter drew up the lease, a month's rent was paid in advance, and the thing was done.

"Well, now, boys, that's off our minds," said Charley gleefully; "my head's been turning round like a buzz-saw ever since this thing's been talked about."

"And a good job, too, seein' as how we skipped without a clearance," Bill put in quietly.

The two friends looked at him blankly, then at each other. It was plain that no such matter had ever entered their minds. Charley gave a long, low whistle. "By George, I never thought of that!" he exclaimed, in great ill humor with Bill. "What 'll they do to us?"

"No use cryin' over spilt milk," said that worthy. "Keep dark 's our lay. Didn't Noah's Ark sail without a clearance, without papers or flag, and for no port?" he added.

"We 'cleared out,' as the sayin' is, with a

vengeance," Charley remarked, trying to turn the matter off with a joke.

" There's only one thing for us to do," said Walter, " and that is to go right up to the custom-house and explain matters to the collector, when we get back to the Bay. Perhaps he'll let us off with a fine, when he finds we didn't mean to run away with the ship and turn pirates."

The idea of turning the old, water-logged *Southern Cross* into a pirate was so comical that all three joined in a hearty laugh.

What to do with all their money was the most perplexing question. They could neither eat nor sleep for thinking of it. In every face they saw a thief, every footstep startled them. In their dilemma it was determined that the safer way would be to divide it up between them. Three miner's belts were therefore procured, and after locking themselves up in the cabin the three friends stuffed these belts as full as they would hold with the precious metal. But there was still a good-sized pile left to be disposed of when this was done, so Bill suggested sewing the remainder in their shirts. At it they went, without more words, sitting meantime in their trousers and undershirts; and a truly comical sight was this original sewing circle, stitching away for dear life under lock and key.

But even when this operation was finished, a heap of the shining metal still lay on the table before them. All were so weighed down with what they had about them that they waddled rather than walked. Bill declared that if anything happened to the boat at their returning they would all sink to the bottom like so much lead. While thus at their wits' end, Charley's eagle eye chanced to fall upon an old fowling piece hung up by some hooks in the cabin. This was quickly torn from its resting place, the charges drawn, and while the others looked on in silent wonder Charley filled both barrels with gold dust, after which the muzzles were tightly fitted with corks. "She's loaded for big game. We take turns carryin' her, don't you see?" he remarked with a broad grin.

Towards dusk the trio took passage on board the first boat bound for the Bay, nor did they feel themselves wholly safe with their treasure until they once more trod the deck of the old *Argonaut*, fairly worn out with a week of such rapidly shifting fortunes as no one but an old Californian has ever experienced.

The three inseparables were snugly rolled up in their blankets, Bill loudly snoring in his bunk, when the distant booming of a gun caused Walter to raise his head and say drowsily, "Hello! a steamer's in."

"I don't care if there's twenty steamers," Charley yawned, at the same time burying his nose still deeper under his blanket; "I was almost gone and now you've made me begin all over again. All ashore that's goin' ashore."

XIX

MR. BRIGHT came in that steamer. As Walter's letter seemed to hold out fair hopes of recovering some part of the *Southern Cross* and her cargo, the merchant had decided to look into the matter himself, though in truth both he and his partners had long regarded the venture as a dead loss.

Had he suddenly dropped from the clouds, the *Argonaut's* little company could not have been more astonished than when the merchant stepped on deck, smiling benignantly at the evident consternation he thus created.

After a hearty greeting all round, though poor Walter turned all colors at the remembrance of how and where they had last met, Mr. Bright began by explaining that he had found them out through the consignee of the *Southern Cross*. " But where in the world is the *Southern Cross?*" he asked. " Here has the boatman been rowing me around for the last hour, trying to find her. Nothing has happened to her, I hope," he hastily added, observing the friends exchanging sly glances.

This question, of course, led to an explanation from Walter, during which the old merchant's face was a study. His first look of annoyance soon changed to one of blank amazement, finally settling down into a broad smile of complete satisfaction when the story was all told. Then he shook his gray head as if the problem was quite too knotty for him to solve, how these boys, hardly out of their teens, should have dared, first to engage in such a brilliant transaction, and then have succeeded in carrying it through to the end without a hitch.

" Pretty well for beginners, I must say," he finally declared. " Taken altogether that's about the boldest operation I ever heard of, and I've known a few in my experience as a business man. But," looking at Walter, "where's all this money? Quite safe, I hope."

By way of answer, the young men brought out their treasure from various ingenious hiding-places, the fowling piece included. When all the belts and parcels of dust were piled in a heap on the table, Mr. Bright sat for some time with his hand over his eyes without speaking. What the merchant's thoughts were it were vain to guess. Finally he said, "You seem to have done everything for the best. Bill here was quite right about the ship. She is earning something where she is, at least. Now about the cargo?" turning to Walter; "I think you said in your letter that Charley here bought half of that in?"

Walter gave a nod of assent.

"Why, then," resumed Mr. Bright, "as the other half belongs to his partner, I don't see that we've anything to do with this money.

Perhaps we may compromise as to the ship," he added, looking at Charley.

Charley then explained his agreement with his partner, who had so mysteriously disappeared. "I sold out to Walter. Settle it with him," he finished, jamming his hands in his pockets and turning away.

"Well, then, Walter, what do you say?"

"I say that Charley ought to have half the profits. Why, when I wrote you, the lumber was worthless. Besides, Charley did all the business. Settle it with him."

"I see. The situation was changed from a matter of a few hundreds to thousands shortly after your letter was written." Walter nodded. "And you don't care to take advantage of it?" Walter simply folded his arms defiantly. "But between you you saved the cargo," the merchant rejoined. "We've no claim. You must come to terms. Was there no writing?"

Walter scowled fiercely at Charley, who, notwithstanding, immediately produced his copy of the agreement. The merchant glanced over it with a smile hovering on his lips.

" Why, this is perfectly good," he declared. " Well, then, as neither of you has a proposition to make, I'll make you one. Perhaps Walter here felt under a moral obligation to look after our interests in spite of the unjust treatment he had received. That I can now understand, and I ask his pardon. But you, Charles, had no such inducement."

" No inducement! " Charley broke out, with a quivering lip; " no inducement, heh, to see that boy righted? " he repeated, struggling hard to keep down the lump in his throat.

" Axin' pardons don't mend no broken crockery," observed Bill gruffly.

Mr. Bright showed no resentment at this plain speech. He sat wiping his glasses in deep thought. Perhaps there was just a little moisture in his own eyes, over this evidence of two hearts linked together as in bands of steel.

The silence was growing oppressive, when Walter nerved himself to say: "You see, sir, Charley and me, we are of one mind. As for me, I'm perfectly satisfied to take what I put in to fit Charley out, provided you pay him back his investment, and what's right for his and Bill's time and trouble."

Charley coughed a little at this liberal proposal, but Walter signed to him to keep quiet. Bill grunted out something that might pass for consent.

But Mr. Bright was not the man to take advantage of so much generosity. In truth, he had already formed in his own mind a plan by which to come to an agreement. Changing the subject for the moment, he suddenly asked, "By the way, have you never heard anything of Ramon?"

At this unexpected question a broad grin stole over the faces of the three kidnapers. "I was coming to that," Walter replied, bringing out from his chest the money and papers which Ramon had been so lately compelled to disgorge. The merchant took them in his hands, ran his eye rapidly over them, and exclaimed in astonishment, " What! did he make this restitution of his own accord? Wonders will never cease, I declare."

" Well, no, sir, not exactly that; the truth is, he was a trifle obstinate about it at first, but we found a way to persuade him. That confession was signed in the very same chair you are now sitting in."

Mr. Bright again said, with a sigh of deep satisfaction, " Marvelous! We shall now pay everything we owe, except our debt to you, Walter; that we can never pay."

" If my good name is cleared, I'm perfectly satisfied," Walter rejoined, a little nervously, yet with a feeling that this was the happiest day of his life.

" And his good name, too, why don't you say?" interrupted the matter-of-fact Bill, from his corner. " Seems to me that's about the size of it," he finished, casting a meaning look at the dignified old merchant, who sat there twiddling his glasses, clearly oppressed by the feeling that, as between himself and Walter, Walter had acted the nobler part. He could hardly control a slight tremor in his voice when he began to speak again.

"I see how it is," he said. "You return good for evil. It was nobly done, I grant you—nobly done. But you must not wonder at my surprise, for I own I expected nothing of the sort. Still, all the generosity must not be on one side. By no means. Since I've sat here I've been thinking that now we are embarked in the California trade, we couldn't do better than to start a branch of the concern in this city. Now, don't interrupt," raising an admonitory hand, "until you hear me through. If you, Walter, and you, Charles, in whom I have every confidence—if you two will accept an equal partnership, your actual expenses to be paid at any rate, we will put all the profits of this lumber trade of yours into the new house to start with. Suppose we call it Bright, Seabury & Company. Fix that to suit yourselves, only my name ought to stand first, I think, because it will set Walter here right before the world."

Neither Walter nor Charley could have said one word for the life of him, so much were they taken by surprise. Bill's eyes fairly bulged out of his shaggy head. Mr. Bright went on to say, " With our credit restored, we can send you all the goods you may want. Suppose we now go and deposit this money—one-half to the new firm's credit, one half in trust for Charles' former partner. I myself will put a notice of the copartnership in to-morrow's papers, and as soon as I get home in the Boston papers, and I should greatly like to see the new sign up before I go."

It was a long speech, but never was one listened to with more rapt attention. Charley turned as red as a beet, Walter hung his head, Bill blew his nose for a full half-minute.

"Where does Bill come in?" he demanded, with a comical side glance at the merchant.

His question, with the long face he put on, relieved the strain at once.

"Oh, never fear, old chap; you shall have my place and pay on the old ship," Charley hastened to assure him.

"Then you accept," said Mr. Bright, shaking hands with each of the new partners in turn. "Something tells me that this is the best investment of my life. The papers shall be made out to-day, while we are looking up a store together. Really, now, I feel as if I ought to give a little dinner in honor of the new firm—long life and prosperity to it! Where shall it be?"

"What ails this 'ere old ship where the old house came to life agin, an' the new babby wuz fust born inter the world?" was Bill's ready suggestion.

"Capital! couldn't be better," exclaimed the merchant. "And now," taking out his notebook, "tell me what I can do for each of you personally when I get back to the States?"

Walter spoke first. "Please look up my old aunty, and see her made comfortable." Mr. Bright jotted down the address with an approving nod, then looked up at Charley.

"Send out a couple of donkey engines; horses are too slow."

Mr. Bright then turned to Bill.

"Me? Oh, well, I've got no aunt, I've no use for donkeys. You might lick that sneakin' perleeceman on the wharf an' send me his resate."

When the two young men took leave of Mr. Bright, on board the *John L. Stephens*, after a hearty hand-shaking all round, that gentleman gave them this parting advice: "Make all the friends you can, and keep them if you can. Remember, nothing is easier than to make enemies."

At a meaning look from Walter, Charley withdrew himself out of earshot. Walter fidgeted a little, blushed, and then managed to ask, " Have I your permission to write to Miss Dora, sir ? "

Mr. Bright looked surprised, then serious, then amused. " Oho! now I begin to catch on. That's how the land lies, is it? So that was the reason why you were prowling around our house one night after dark, was it? Well, well! Certainly you may write to Dora. And by the way, when next you pass through our street you may ring the doorbell."

XX

Thus the new firm entered upon its future career with bright prospects. A suitable warehouse on the waterfront was leased for a term of years. True to their determination to stick together, the two junior partners fitted up a room in the second story, and on the day that the doors were first opened for business they moved in. The next thing was to get some business to do.

Charley had a considerable acquaintance among the ranchmen across the Bay, which he now improved by making frequent trips to solicit consignments of country produce. The sight of an empty store and bare walls was at first depressing, but their first shipments from the East could not be expected for sev-

eral months.   There was a sort of tacit understanding that Walter should attend to the
financial end of the business, while Charley
took care of the outdoor concerns.   They
were no longer boys.   The sense of assumed
responsibilities had made them men.

The two partners were busy receiving a
sloop-load of potatoes, with their shirt
sleeves rolled up, when a big, burly, be-
whiskered individual dropped in upon them.
Scenting a customer, Charley, always forward, briskly asked what they could do for
him.

" I want to see the senior partner."

Charley nodded toward Walter, who was
checking off the weights.

The man gave a quick look at the tall,
straight young fellow before him, then said,
" Can I speak to you in private for five
minutes ? "

" Come this way," Walter replied, showing the stranger into the little office.

The newcomer sat down, crossed one leg

over the other, stroked his long beard reflectively a little, and said, " I've come on a very confidential matter. Can I depend upon the strictest privacy? "

" You may," said Walter, quite astonished at this rather unexpected opening. " Nobody will interrupt us here."

The man cast an inquisitive look around, as if to make sure there were no eavesdroppers near, then, lowering his voice almost to a whisper, said pointedly, " You may have heard something about a plan to aid the poor, oppressed natives of Nicaragua to throw off the tyrannical yoke of their present rulers? "

" I've seen something to that effect in the papers," said Walter evasively.

" So much the better. That clears the way of cobwebs. I want your solemn promise that what passes between us shall not be divulged to a human being."

" I have no business secrets from my partners," Walter objected.

" Your partners! Oh! of course not."

" I've already promised," Walter assented, more and more mystified by the stranger's manner. " Nobody asked you for your secrets. You can do as you like about telling them," he continued rather sharply.

" I'll trust you. You are a young concern. Well connected. Bang-up references. Likely to get on top of the heap, and nat'rally want to make a strike. Nothing like seizing upon a golden opportunity. ' There is a tide '— you know the rest. Now, I'm just the man to put you in the way of doing it, as easy as rolling off a log."

As Walter made no reply, the visitor, after waiting a moment for his words to take effect, went on: " Now, listen. I don't mind telling you, in the strictest confidence, then, that I'm fiscal agent for this here enterprise. I'm in it for glory and the *dinero*. We want some enterprising young firm like yours to furnish supplies for the emigrants we're sending down there," jerking his head toward the south. " There's a big pile in it for you, if you will take hold with us and see the thing through."

Walter kept his eyes upon the speaker, but said nothing.

" You see, it's a perfectly legitimate transaction, don't you? " resumed the fiscal agent a little anxiously.

" Then why so much secrecy? "

" Oh! there's always a lot of people prying round into what don't concern them. Busybodies! If it gets out that our people aren't peaceable emigrants before we're good and ready, the whole thing might get knocked into a cocked hat. They'd say—well, they even might call us filibusters," the man admitted with an injured air.

Walter smiled a knowing smile. " What do you want us to do? " he asked.

" In the first place, we want cornmeal, hard bread, bacon, potatoes, an' sich, for a hundred and fifty men for two months. I can give you the figures to a dot," the agent rejoined, on whom Walter's smile had not been lost.

"See here." He drew out of his pocket a package of freshly printed bonds, purporting to be issued by authority of the Republic of Nicaragua, and passed them over for Walter's inspection. "Now, the fact is, we want all our ready funds for the people's outfit, advance money, vessel's charter, and so on. Now, I'm going to be liberal with you. I'll put up this bunch of twenty thousand dollars in bonds, payable on the day Nicaragua is free, for five thousand dollars' worth of provisions at market price. Think of that! Twenty thousand dollars for five thousand dollars. You can't lose. We've got things all fixed down there. Why, man, there's silver and gold and jewels enough in the churches alone to pay those bonds ten times over!"

"What! rob the churches!" Walter exclaimed, knitting his brows.

"Why, no; I believe they call that merely a forced loan nowadays," objected the fiscal agent in some embarrassment.

Seeing that he paused for a reply, Walter observed that he would consult his partner. Charley was called in and the proposal gone over again with him. As soon as advised of its purport he turned on his heel.

"Not any in mine," was his prompt decision.

"Mine either," assented Walter.

The stranger seemed much disappointed, but not yet at the end of his resources. "Well, then," he began again, "you take the bonds, sell them for a fair discount for cash, and use the proceeds towards those provisions?"

"Hadn't you better do that yourself? We're not brokers. We're commission merchants. If you come to us with cash in hand we'll sell you anything money will buy, and no questions asked; but Nicaragua bonds, payable any time and no time, are not in our line." So said Walter.

"Not much," echoed Charley.

"Your line seems to be small potatoes,"

muttered the stranger testily. Then quickly checking himself, he carelessly asked, " I suppose you'd have no objection to keeping these bonds in your safe for a day or two for me, giving me a receipt for them, or the equivalent? I don't feel half easy about carrying them about with me."

" Why, no," said Charley, looking at Walter, to see how he would take it.

" Yes," objected Walter, "most decidedly."

" ' No;' 'yes;' who's boss here, anyhow? " sneered the agent, dimissing his wheedling tone, now that he had played his last card. Even Charley seemed a trifle nettled at being snubbed by Walter in the presence of a stranger. After all, it seemed a trifling favor to ask of them.

" My partner and I can settle that matter between ourselves. Once for all, we don't choose to be mixed up in your filibustering schemes in any way. Your five minutes have grown to three-quarters of an hour already.

This is our busy day," he concluded, as a broad hint to the stranger to take leave, and at once.

" Very well," said the unmoved fiscal agent, buttoning up his coat. " But you'll repent, all the same, having thrown away the finest opportunity of making a fortune ever offered——"

" This way out, sir," Charley interrupted, throwing wide the office door.

When the strange visitor had gone Charley asked Walter why he refused to let the bonds be put in the safe. " Now we've made an enemy," he said resignedly.

" To let him raise money on that receipt for twenty thousand dollars, *or equivalent*—on Mr. Bright's name? No, sir-ee. Where were your wits, Charles Wormwood? That fellow's a sharper! "

" Guess I'd better attend to those potatoes," was all the junior partner could find to say, suiting the action to the word.

As was quite natural, much curiosity was

felt as to what had become of Ramon, by his former business associates. In some way he had found out that Mr. Bright was in San Francisco, and taking counsel of his fears of being sent back to Boston as a confessed felon, he cast his lot among the most lawless adventurers of the day. Learning that a filibustering expedition was being fitted out at San Francisco against Lower California, under command of Walker, the " Gray-eyed Man of Destiny," Ramon joined it, keeping in hiding meanwhile, until the vessel was ready to sail. As is well known, the affair was a complete failure, Walker's famished band being compelled to surrender to the United States officers at San Diego. From this time Ramon disappeared.

  .   .   .   .   .

Some five years later a young man, ruddy-cheeked, robust, and well though not foppishly dressed, drove up to the door of a pretty cottage in one of the most fashionable suburbs of Boston. Alighting from his buggy and hitching his horse, he walked quickly up the driveway to the house. The front door flew open by the time he had put his hand on the knob; and a young woman, with the matchless New England pink and white in her cheeks, called out, " Why, Walter, what brings you home so early to-day? Has anything happened? "

" Yes, Dora; Charles Wormwood is coming out to dine with us to-day. He only arrived to-day overland. I want to show him my wife."

THE END

A STORY OF REAL BOYS AND FOR THEM

By MARTHA JAMES

Square 12mo   Cloth   Illustrated by FRANK T. MERRILL   200 pages $1.00

As a sub-title to her latest book for young people, " My Friend Jim," Martha James has added the line " A Story of Real Boys and for Them," and it is a real book in the best sense of the word. As a testimony as to what one real boy at least thinks of it it may not be out of place to relate a little incident which occurred Christmas week.

Having missed one of the boys of the household, a lad given more to baseball and shinney than books, the writer was surprised to find him lying at full-length on a big rug before the fire in the library, deep in a book.

" Hello ! what are you reading? " was the exclamatory question.

" ' My Friend Jim,' " was the brief reply.

" Is it good ? "

" Well, I guess ; it's a dandy ! " and with an impatient gesture that indicated that he did not want to be further interrupted, he turned his back toward his questioner and buried his face in his book.

Jim is a country boy, strong and healthy in mind and body, though poor and humble, whose companionship is the means of improving physically, as well as broadening in mind and character, the invalid son of a man of means forced to remain abroad on business. Brandt, the city boy, spends the summer in the country near Jim's home, and the simple adventures and pleasures of the lads form the interest of the story. — *Brooklyn Citizen.*

LEE and SHEPARD Boston

Made in the USA
San Bernardino, CA
03 January 2020

62579145R00166